Sometimes you can't see the magic.
You just know it's there because you can feel it.

PRAISE FOR *TORTILLA SUN*:

"A beautiful and engaging debut novel."
—*Kirkus Reviews*

"[A] strong debut. . . . an imaginative
yet grounded novel."
—*Publishers Weekly*

"Cervantes' first novel is rich with local color—both
physical landscapes and traditional spiritual beliefs."
—*Booklist*

TORTILLA SUN

JENNIFER CERVANTES

chronicle books · san francisco

First paperback edition published in 2014 by Chronicle Books LLC.
Originally published in hardcover in 2010 by Chronicle Books LLC.

ISBN 978-1-4521-3150-4

The Library of Congress has cataloged the original edition as follows:
Cervantes, Jennifer.
Tortilla sun / by Jennifer Cervantes.
p. cm.
Summary: While spending a summer in New Mexico with her grandmother,
twelve-year-old Izzy makes new friends, learns to cook, and for the first time hears
stories about her father, who died before she was born.
ISBN 978-0-8118-7015-3 (alk. paper)
[1. Fathers and daughters—Fiction. 2. Grandmothers—Fiction. 3. New Mexico—Fiction.] I. Title.
PZ7.C3198Tor 2010
[Fic]—dc22
2009029620

Manufactured in China.

MIX
Paper from
responsible sources
FSC
www.fsc.org
FSC™ C144853

Interior Book design by Natalie Davis.
Cover illustration by Jolby & Friends.
Cover design by Kristine Brogno.
Typeset in FF Scala and Old Claude LP.

10 9 8 7 6 5

Chronicle Books LLC
680 Second Street, San Francisco, California 94107

Chronicle Books—we see things differently.
Become part of our community at www.chroniclekids.com.

For my daughters, Alex, Bella, and Jules.
I love you more than all the stars in the sky.

PROLOGUE

EL CUENTITO

This is a *cuento*, a story about magic, love, hope, and treasure. If you read this under the glow of the moon or by the light of the summer sun, listen for whispers in any breeze that passes by. Then close your eyes and let the *cuento* take you to where magic still exists and spells of fear and hope are told through the heart of the storyteller.

1

THE MAGIC BASEBALL

I stared at the glossy image. Six-year-old toothless me holding Mom's hand as white waves broke on the shore behind us. A strand of dark hair blew in Mom's face, hiding what might have been a small smile.

I turned as Mom appeared in the doorway. "Look at this. I was so little." I held up the picture, smiling.

When Mom's eyes found the box I had opened, confusion swept across her face. "Where did you find that? I thought we'd unpacked everything."

"It . . . was in here," I said.

She stepped into the spare room of our new apartment. We'd moved all over San Diego. From 4th Street to 10th Street and from Mulberry Road to Elm Road. The last place we lived was on Paradise Place. That had a nice ring to it. Now, we were living at 1423 M Street. "M" for *maybe* this will finally be home.

"I haven't seen this in ages." Her eyes danced as she traced her long fingers over the photo. "I think you had just lost that front tooth." She chuckled at the memory.

A soft breeze crawled in through the window, tickling my face. That's when I caught sight of something else in the box.

A baseball.

I took the baseball from the box and rotated it in my hand. The words *because* and *magic* were written across the front. "Whose is this?"

Mom looked up and yanked the ball from my grasp.

"Wait. I want to look at it. What do those words mean?" I said.

"I . . . It's nothing. Help me fold up this box."

"Is it Dad's?" I asked barely above a whisper.

Mom turned to me. "I said never mind, Izzy. It's just an old nothing." But I knew it wasn't a nothing. Dad died before I was born and Mom never wanted to talk about him. But I imagined we were just the same. That he hated moving from place to place, never finding a home. I bet he hated packing too, unless it was for vacation.

Mom grabbed the box and marched down the hall. I heard the closet door slam. Then she reappeared and leaned against the doorframe. "We don't need to unpack that one. Just leave it alone. "

"But . . ."

She put her palm up. "I said leave it alone."

That night, I sat at my desk beneath the window to write down some ideas for a story. "Because magic," I whispered. Did my dad write those words? And why was there a gap between the words like something was missing?

The June moon hung low in the sky like it was attached to some invisible string. Its brilliant yellow light filtered through the palms outside, creating dancing shadows on the bare white walls of my room.

I tapped a pen against my cheek and stared at a blank index card. I had a whole stack of them with the beginnings of my unfinished stories. Mrs. Barney, my fifth grade teacher, had turned me on to them. She said small cards weren't so intimidating for "budding writers." I'd asked her what budding meant; she just laughed and told me I was growing.

But what did me being tall have to do with writing? I doodled little hearts on the card while I thought about a new story. *One day, a girl named Sara . . .* No, not Sara. Something more interesting.

Pushing my long dark hair from my face, I grazed my silver hoop earring and stared at the empty moving boxes on the floor. *Gypsy.* Yes, *a girl named Gypsy.*

I scribbled the beginning of the story.

One day Gypsy opened a secret box. Inside she found a ball. And . . . And what? With my pen in hand, I leaned back and spun my swivel chair in slow circles. "That's it!" I said.

And it was magic. It . . .

I scratched out the word *it* and wrote:

But her mother said the ball was worthless and buried it.

"Where would she bury *it,*" I whispered. "Maybe in the backyard?" No, Gypsy lived somewhere amazing, like a castle. *Her mother buried it in an orchard outside the castle walls.* But why would her mother bury the ball? What was she hiding?

Frustrated, I laid my head on the desk. I was good at starting a story. It was the finishing that was hard. Like trying to finish a puzzle without all the pieces.

When the phone rang, I snapped upright. Mom answered before the second ring like she was expecting the call. I tiptoed toward the closed bedroom door. Who could be calling this late? I quietly opened my door and pressed my ear to the crack. Mom's voice, coming from the living room, was hushed.

"No I haven't told her yet. I will."

Silence.

"Maybe this will be good for her. I just worry . . . she is bound to find the truth and—"

Mom sighed at this point, and I pictured her rubbing her hand back and forth across her forehead. "I know. Maybe it's the best way. Do you think she'll forgive me?"

Can't talk about what? Forgive her for what?

"If she asks, take it slow." Mom paused for a long minute then whispered something into the phone I didn't catch because a car horn honked right outside my window. The last thing I heard was, "Thanks, Mama."

Nana? Why was she talking to Nana? She hardly ever talked to her. All of a sudden the night felt heavy.

I glanced back at my story card and imagined Gypsy sneaking into the orchard to unbury the ball while her mother slept. I told myself if I could get the ball without waking Mom, it would be a sign that it was meant to be mine. And if I didn't, it would stay locked away.

Finally after half an hour, I heard Mom close her bedroom door.

I inched toward my bedroom door and slowly pressed it open. I could hear the low hum of distant traffic as I stood waiting in my doorway. I counted to one hundred slowly, achingly, then crept into the hall.

The wind outside pushed against the walls, making them creak and groan. I opened the closet door directly across from Mom's bedroom and quietly climbed onto the bottom shelf to reach the box at the top. Reaching my arm inside, I pushed through stacks of paper until my fingers brushed the long, bumpy stitches of the baseball.

ONE WISH

*C*lang cla-clang, clang clang. The next morning, I found Mom in the kitchen with a chisel and hammer, chipping away at the kitchen counter. Little flecks of white flew through the air like ceramic snow, landing softly on her olive-colored cheeks.

I ducked as a piece of tile flew at me. "Hey!"

She turned toward me with a look of surprise. "Morning, Izzy. I didn't see you standing there."

"Wha . . . what are you doing?" I asked.

She stepped back and surveyed the half-demolished counter the way someone stands back to study a newly hung photograph. Wiping her cheek with the back of her hand she said, "There was this"—she searched the mess on the floor—"this one broken tile poking out and I thought I should fix it and . . ."

I pushed past her to get the broom but she grabbed me by the elbow. A feeling of nervousness swelled inside me.

"Izzy, wait. I have something to tell you."

There it was. My heart buckled in my chest. Something was wrong.

Mom leaned back against the counter and sucked in a great gulp of air. "It's strange actually. I wasn't expecting it, but then at the last minute the funding came through." She folded her arms across her waist. "I'm going to Costa Rica to finish my research."

Her words buzzed around me like a swarm of confused bees. "When? For how long?"

"I'll be gone for most of the summer. I leave Tuesday."

Mom wouldn't leave me. We'd go together. Right? "But that's only three days away." I stepped away from Mom and the shards of tile.

"I don't have a choice."

"But what am I supposed to do? That's three whole months."

"Two. I'll be home at the end of July. And after this I can finally graduate. Our lives will change then." She reached over and stroked my hair. "For the better."

I rolled those three words around in my mind: *for the better.*

Suddenly last night's phone call made perfect sense. I inched closer and pushed at the broken tile with my toes.

"Are you sending me to Nana's?" I asked. "In New Mexico?"

A flash of surprise crossed Mom's face. Like she knew I had heard her phone conversation. "She's so excited to have you and . . ."

"What happened to all your talk about you guys not seeing eye to eye?" I asked.

"It's not that we don't see eye to eye. We just don't see the world the same way."

"Why can't I go with you?" I said.

"Izzy . . ."

"New Mexico is worlds away from California. And what am I going to do for two whole months with someone I haven't seen since I was six? That was half my life ago. She's a stranger!" I felt a sudden urge to bolt for the front door and run.

Mom rolled her eyes. "Oh, Izzy. She's hardly a stranger. She's family. I already have your ticket. You leave Monday." Mom opened the refrigerator and took out a diet soda, pressing the cold can against her face before opening it.

I stared at the mess on the floor. "Why can't I stay here? Alone." My voice quivered.

Mom took a swig of her soda, then closed her eyes and took a deep breath. When she opened them, she spoke slowly and deliberately.

"You're going to New Mexico and that's final."

I swallowed hard and tried not to cry. "Why do you always get to decide everything? We just unpacked and I—I had plans."

She raised her eyebrows, surprised. "Plans?"

Mom was always bugging me to make friends, which I didn't see the point of, considering we moved every few months. And we moved for all sorts of reasons: closer to the university for her, better school for me, quieter, prettier, bigger, smaller.

"I was going to try and find some girls my age here in the complex so I wouldn't have to be the new kid in school *again*," I said, trying to sound believable.

"Honey, you can make friends at your new school in the fall. Besides, this is a wonderful opportunity for you."

"Opportunity? For me? Or for you?"

I stormed off to my room and threw myself onto my bed. I ached inside. Like the feeling you get watching a lost balloon float far into the sky until it becomes an invisible nothing.

I reached for a story card and scribbled:

Gypsy was sent to prison for stealing the magic ball. And when she was tossed into the dungeon below the castle she found the word "opportunity" written across the stone wall.

Staring at the card, I wondered what should happen next. Maybe a daring escape or a sorceress could rescue her. When nothing came to me, I scratched out the word *opportunity* until it was a big blob of blue ink and tossed the card on the floor.

I heard Mom's footsteps coming toward my closed bedroom door. I held my breath, hoping she wouldn't knock.

Tap. Tap.

Silence.

"Izzy?" she spoke quietly.

My hands wandered beneath my pillow and gripped the baseball I had hidden there. I squeezed my eyes closed and whispered, "I wish I didn't have to go. I wish I didn't have to go."

"I've brought your suitcase." She stood outside my door for what seemed like forever. I pictured her on the other side, arms crossed, head down.

"I think you're going to like the village." Her voice became a little muffled now, like her mouth was pressed right up against the door. "It's strange and beautiful at the same time and a perfect place to explore. You just might be surprised what you find there." She paused for a moment then continued. "Would you please talk to me?"

I burrowed my head under the pillow with the baseball. A tiny piece of me felt guilty for stealing it, but it belonged to my dad and that made it special. That made it a part of me.

"I'll just leave the suitcase here for you," she said. Her bare feet slapped against the tile and carried her away.

3

BIENVENIDA

Two days later, I stood at the gate waiting to board the plane. Mom adjusted my backpack and smiled anxiously. "It will go by fast, really."

I didn't know if she was trying to convince me or herself. I stared at the purple and blue threads zigzagging through the carpet and wondered why my wish hadn't come true.

Mom squeezed me tight and pushed my hair from my face. "I'll see you soon."

I nodded and handed my boarding pass to the agent. I didn't look back.

From thousands of feet in the air, Albuquerque looked like brown sandpaper stretched between a giant mountain in the east and a long green ribbon of trees in the west. The river beyond the valley curled back and forth across the landscape as if it were looking for a place to rest. I squeezed my eyes shut and felt my stomach churn as the plane drew closer to this strange place.

Moments after I got off the airplane and walked into the airport, I noticed a small man in a straw cowboy hat holding a sign that read "Isadora Roybal." I looked around for Nana. I had a small picture of her in my backpack just in case I couldn't remember what she looked like. As I approached, the man smiled.

The brim of his hat met my eyebrows and made me feel too tall for my age, like a flamingo on stilts.

"*Hola, señorita.* You must be Isadora."

"Izzy," I said.

His black almond eyes drooped at the corners and only turned up when he smiled, which he couldn't seem to stop doing. He reached for my small suitcase. "I am Mr. Castillo, your ride home."

Why would Nana send some stranger to pick me up? Maybe she didn't really want me for the summer. I pulled my suitcase closer. "Where's my nana?"

"Cooking for the *fiesta*."

I could tell he expected me to follow him but I stood still, unsure of what to do next.

"Maybe I should call her first," I said.

He laughed. "Yes. I agree. Except she won't answer the phone when she is cooking. *Mira*, I can prove she sent me and I am who I say I am." He took off his hat, as if this might help him think better.

I nodded.

"Your name is Isadora." He smiled. "I mean Izzy Roybal, age twelve, a true New Mexican." He put his hat back on his head. "And your mama is Maria Roybal."

I twisted my hair around my finger. "What else do you know about me?"

"More details?" He laughed.

"You have your mother's chin, and strong will, but your eyes remind me of your papa, as if he were standing here before me."

"You knew my father?"

"Everyone in the village knew him. Jack was a very good man. You should feel proud to be his daughter."

If he was so good, why did Mom keep him from me?

"Now, *ven*. Your nana is busy preparing for you. Let's not disappoint her."

He turned and led me outside to a rusted pickup truck filled to the brim with yellow onions. The hot, dry air scraped against my skin just like the words Mr. Castillo said about my dad scratched at a corner of my mind.

"You must really like onions," I said.

"*Sí*. But these are for sale. I grow them." He smiled proudly.

I slid into the cab of the truck beside him and clutched my backpack on my lap. Soon we rolled onto the highway. The truck whizzed by sunburned earth dotted with dark green bushes too scrawny to provide any shade. Mountains loomed ahead in the distance as we sped down the highway.

"Those are the Sandia mountains," Mr. Castillo said as we drew closer. "*Sandía* means watermelon in Spanish. *¿Hablas español?*"

"I understand a little Spanish but my mom never really taught me. And they don't look like watermelons."

He chuckled. "Wait until sunset. They will turn the most beautiful pink you've ever seen."

As we drove, each mile of desert seemed the same as the mile before.

"What are those?" I pointed toward the sky in the distance.

"Haven't you ever seen a hot air balloon?"

"Only in the movies," I said.

He laughed. "People come from all over come to ride our skies. They say our wind is perfect."

"Can anyone ride in them?" I asked.

Mr. Castillo rubbed the back of his neck. "You know come to think of it, the village has a balloon. Or used to." His voice softened. "Don't know whatever happened to it."

"What is the village like?"

Mr. Castillo glanced sideways at me. "I forget, you've not been since you were a baby. Well then, you will have to see for yourself."

He smiled and bounced in his seat to the rhythm of the Mexican music on the radio. My heart skipped off-key as I wiped my sweaty palms across my jeans. Where was Mom sending me?

By the time we reached the edge of the village, more than forty miles away, I had sneezed no fewer than twenty times and I could feel my eyelids swelling to the size of grapes. But I felt a pinch of hope as we crisscrossed back roads toward a lush valley where majestic trees crowned the sienna earth.

The truck bounced down a dirt road lined with *adobe* homes on both sides. The roofs were flat and the walls had thick rounded edges that made them look like packed mud.

Mr. Castillo stopped and pointed to the left as we approached a plaza bracketed with big, full trees and bordered by more *adobes*. "That's the village center."

A big round lady stooped over a crying boy with dark brown cheeks. He'd spilled his chocolate ice cream cone on his shoe. Two little girls in sundresses chased a Chihuahua across the grass as it darted toward the melting chocolate. To our right, stone steps led to a small *adobe* church with large cracks down its walls. Mr. Castillo made the sign of the cross as we passed.

"Is this where Nana lives?"

He shook his head. "She lives a couple of miles from the center, out in the quiet country."

We started down a long dirt road lined with cottonwood and elm trees. A large *adobe* house with windows trimmed in bright turquoise lay at the end. Tree limbs bowed over the sides of the flat roof, screening out the hot New Mexico sun, and the house stretched from one edge of the shade to the next.

I hopped down from the pickup, tossed my backpack over my right shoulder, and followed Mr. Castillo through a crooked wooden gate that lead into a sunny courtyard. I had to be careful not to trip over all the terracotta pots filled with vibrant yellow-and-purple wildflowers lining the narrow brick pathway leading to the front door.

"Ah, *mijita!*" Nana burst from the front door and knocked over a small wooden statue of Mary. She swept past the statue as Mr. Castillo knelt down to pick it up. I didn't remember her being so small.

She reached up and hugged me tight. "Isadora, you've grown like the elm."

My body stiffened under her embrace. "Just Izzy."

She stepped back and gazed at me, smiling. "Your mama sent pictures but they didn't show me how *bonita* you are! *Ay*, you are so big. I haven't seen you since that last trip to California." She tapped her fingers on the side of her face like she were counting the years. "Do you remember? You must've been only six or so." She waved her hand in the air. "Yes, I could never live in such a busy place. Too much traffic and so many people."

Her small round frame made me feel even taller than the flamingo on stilts.

She turned to Mr. Castillo. "*Gracias.*"

He removed his hat and leaned forward. "*De nada.*"

Then he leaned toward me and said with a warm smile, "*Bienvenida.* Welcome."

"Come, come—meet my *amigas*," Nana said, bouncing toward the front door. Her rose colored dress nearly covered her small bare feet.

We made our way inside where a dozen women stood on each side of a long pine table, laughing and pressing their hands into big, silver mixing bowls.

"We are making fresh *tamales* for tomorrow's *fiesta*."

"*Fiesta?*"

"*Sí. Mañana* is my best friend's birthday and you're here. Two reasons to celebrate."

Inside, I stood frozen like the Mary statue in Nana's courtyard, staring into a kaleidoscope of colors—red rugs, purple pillows, pink flowers, and yellow walls. My stomach spun like a carousel going too fast and suddenly I ached for home where everything felt familiar. All the women waved and smiled.

"I didn't know you lived out in the country," I said as I wrapped my arms around my aching stomach and did my best to smile back at the strangers.

"This isn't the country, just a small village on the outside of the *ciudad*." She wrinkled up her nose. "And you smell like you just crawled out of a wet onion sack."

"It's the onions from the truck; my throat still burns. I think I must be allergic or something."

"*Sígame*," she said laughing.

I followed her past the long tables and into the sky-blue kitchen. Dried flowers and plants hung in tied bunches from the ceiling, making the kitchen smell like a freshly lit cranberry candle. Nana pinched a few of the bundles between her fingers and ground up the dried flowers into a black stone bowl. Then she poured hot water over the mixture into a teacup.

"Here, drink this." She handed me the tea and a *tortilla* from a basket shaped like a straw hat. "And eat this."

The hot tea slid down my throat, warming everything on the way down. It tasted bitter, like peeling an orange with your teeth, so I took big bites out of the *tortilla*, which made it easier to swallow. I rolled the leftover bits of herbs around in my mouth, not sure if I was supposed to eat those too. But I didn't want to have an allergic reaction to onions ever again, so I pushed the bitterness to the back of my throat and swallowed hard.

4

THE WHISPERING WIND

Nana's whole house seemed to be breathing with color and life. Everywhere I turned, angels and saints stared at me from the walls.

"You sure have a lot of paintings," I said as Nana walked me down a long narrow hall to show me my bedroom.

"*Sí*. These have been in the family for generations. Each has a story."

Nana paused in front of a small painting of Mary holding Baby Jesus that hung on the wall next to a large wooden door. I stood to the left of the painting and then swayed to the right. Mary's eyes followed me back and forth.

"See this painting of Mary? My *papa's papa* received it as a gift from a priest who painted it close to one hundred years ago. It has seen many sorrows and joys. And now it hangs on this wall, protecting all who sleep in this room."

Why would I need protection? I felt light-headed. So many new things spun around me; I wasn't sure what to focus on first. Nana pressed open the door. "Meet Estrella."

A tall four-poster bed stood at the center of the room. Creamy gauze curtains hung loosely around the edges. At the foot of the bed lay a light blue blanket threaded with lemon yellow that matched the blue swirls layering the walls. Two French doors opened to a walled courtyard with a brightly painted yellow and purple fountain.

"It's so . . . so colorful," I said with a hint of surprise.

Nana laughed and leaned against one of the bedposts "But of course it's colorful. Life is color, isn't it?"

I glanced around the room waiting for someone to appear. "So where's Estrella?"

Nana swept her arm in front of her. "The room is named Estrella. See those windows?"

A few inches below the ceiling were two small square windows. But you couldn't see anything out of them unless you wanted to stare at the empty sky.

"Those windows were specially designed, to frame the view of the stars. And star in Spanish is . . ." Nana raised her eyebrows waiting for my reply.

"*Estrella?*" I said.

She nodded. "*Muy bien.*"

I gazed out those windows imagining the stars that would come to visit, but in the light of day all I saw were layers of clouds inching across a lonely blue sky.

"Do you name all the rooms in your house?"

"Only if the name feels right." Nana pressed her small hands on her hips. A warm smile spread across her face.

"Feel free to explore the village," she said as she turned to leave. "It's an enchanting place." She closed the door behind her.

That was the same word Mom had used.

A silent breeze rolled in through the screen of the French doors, brushing my cheeks. Water splashed over the bowl of the small stone fountain beyond.

I unzipped the small pocket on the side of my backpack and took out the baseball that I'd kept hidden for the last few days, in case Mom found it and took it away.

On one side of the ball, little red stitches made an upside down *U* that narrowed at the center and looped wide open again on the other side. At the center, the words *because* and *magic* were written in script, one word stacked on top of the other. But there was this strange empty space about an inch wide between the two words, and when I looked closely I noticed the tiniest of smudges, like some words were missing.

Judging by the size of the handwriting, I counted out how many letters I thought might fit in the small space. Maybe six or seven? It was almost as frustrating as trying to finish a story. Maybe it wasn't even good for wishing anymore with the words rubbed out, but it was still my dad's and I had a feeling that those missing words mattered.

With the ball in hand, I stepped into the courtyard and walked past the fountain onto a small lawn that led to a rose garden. Past the roses, a small slope cascaded down to a grove of trees that seemed to go on forever. Shadows danced and played beneath the swaying branches in the setting sun.

I tossed the ball up, up toward the wispy clouds beyond the treetops. And with a rush it fell back down from the sky. The weight of the ball dropping into my hands felt safe and solid, giving me confidence. So I skipped the ball off a few tree trunks and ran to scoop it up. But with one poorly aimed throw, it bounced into a nearby bush. I dropped on all fours to search for it, but couldn't see much in the shadows of the grove.

"Where are you?" I murmured.

When I stretched my arm into the tangled underbrush, it got caught in the branches. "Ouch!" I removed my arm swiftly and surveyed the small scrapes across my wrist and elbow. Getting the baseball out wasn't going to be so easy. I plunked down at the foot of a large cottonwood, took a deep breath, and closed my eyes. A light breeze caressed my cuts. Drifting off, I heard whispers bounce off the trees, and had a strange feeling I wasn't alone.

Whoosh, whoosh.

After the faintest *whoosh*, one word echoed clearly across the grove: *Come.*

I pressed my back against the tree and scanned the area.

"Who's there?" I called.

Come . . .

The breeze wrapped itself around me. I started to make a run for it but then I remembered my baseball nudged under that nasty bush. I couldn't bear the thought of leaving it there, not overnight. Just as I was about to reach into the thorny branches again, it rolled out from under the bush on its own. In one swift motion, I snatched it up and dashed back toward Nana's, hoping and praying there was enough sunlight to lead the way. My feet raced over the lawn and the breeze followed me. Only when I reached the house and bolted Estrella's French doors behind me did I exhale at last, my hot breath fogging up the glass.

I darted into the hall to grab Mary's picture from the wall. Back in the room, I propped the painting up against the French doors, figuring she'd be better protection from whatever was outside in the trees than a little lock.

"You're back," Nana said from the doorway. "Is everything okay?"

I whipped around, clutching my chest. "You surprised me. Oh yeah, just tired. Thought I'd go to sleep."

Nana glanced toward Mary against the French doors and back toward me.

"I . . . I was just looking at it more closely."

"You are welcome to anything in this house, *mija*." Nana's soft caramel eyes glistened.

Glancing out the window, I nodded slowly.

"I left a burrito by the bed if you're hungry." She tilted her head to one side and stared intently at me. "I am so happy you are finally here. Let me know if you need anything." She turned to leave. "Breakfast is at seven o'clock sharp."

"In the morning?"

Nana laughed and closed the door.

Sinking into the chair at the desk with flaking green paint, I flipped through my story cards until I found a blank one and wrote, *Gypsy found an enchanted forest where the wind spoke to her.*

If Mom were here she would have said, "Be reasonable, Izzy. There must be a logical reason why you heard a voice in the wind."

I repeated the word *logical* over and over as I tried to piece together the events of the day, and that's when I remembered the herbs I ate with the tea. Maybe they had a strange effect on people who weren't used to them, like making them think they heard things.

A few moments later I lay in bed listening to the silence. I longed for the familiar sounds of home: the low hum of traffic, beeping horns, the distant buzz of the street lights. Wedges of moonlight shone across the wall above my bed where an angel statue hung. He had small delicate glass eyes that stared down at me, and one wing stretching upward. I'd never seen an angel with a missing wing. Starlight danced across the angel's face and for just a moment I didn't feel so alone.

And I soon realized I wasn't, because I heard a hushed male voice coming from the walls. I sat up and strained to hear, but couldn't make out the words. I slipped from bed and tiptoed toward a long turquoise Indian rug hanging near the closet. Behind it was a padlocked door. I pressed my ear against it.

"Who's there?" the stranger's voice said.

I jerked back, unsure of what to do. Settled on waking Nana, I turned and headed toward the hall when I heard, "How about some music?" and then a guitar strummed softly. A sweet melody drifted through the walls, filling the room with a steady rhythm that slowed my feet and quieted my mind.

"Who are you?" I whispered as I climbed into bed.

5

PINK AND JOY AND THE GUY BEHIND THE WALL

The next morning, sweet smells floated under the bedroom door, urging me to get up. I blinked at the clock on my nightstand: 6:45.

I shuffled to the kitchen and found Nana swaying to the Spanish ballads on the radio. Her soft yellow dress swayed with her, nearly sweeping the floor. Another woman sat at the kitchen table drinking coffee. The woman winked at me and smiled.

"You must be Isadora." She had a thick Spanish accent, and had on her "painted face," as Mom would have said. Thick black pencil lined her upper eyelids and her lips were filled in past their natural line with orange lipstick that matched her bright orange sundress dotted with little pink roses.

"Izzy," I said as I tried to straighten my messy hair by tucking it behind my ears.

I pictured myself on top of the roof shouting to the whole village: Newsflash. My name is Izzy, NOT Isadora!

Nana turned down the music. "*Buenos días, mijita.* This is Mrs. Castillo. Her husband is the one who brought you home yesterday."

"Nice to meet you, Mrs. Castillo." I sat next to her at the long pine table in the middle of the kitchen.

She waved her arms vigorously. "No, no, no. You call me Tía."

I didn't know much Spanish but I knew enough to know *tía* meant aunt and that she wasn't my aunt.

She must've read my mind. "All the kids in the village call me Tía. It sounds so much younger than Mrs., don't you think?"

I nodded to be polite before a yawn slipped out.

Nana chuckled. "Your mama was never an early riser either. She used to show up in her robe just like you, hair all tousled about her face. Half the time she had her eyes closed."

I raised my eyebrows in surprise. "Well, she's changed a lot then. She usually leaves the house before I'm even up for school."

"Well, who feeds you?"

"Nana, I'm twelve years old. I can pour myself some cereal."

Nana shook her head. "Not in this house. No siree. You will eat home-cooked *comida* every day. No wonder you're just skin and bones."

I felt swallowed by my robe all of a sudden and pulled the tie around my waist tighter.

Mrs. Castillo set her coffee cup on the table and examined her long red nails, then turned her attention back to Nana. "Did you hear Ramona is quitting the church?"

Nana spun around. "Really?"

Mrs. Castillo nodded. "It's that man she's been dating. The old coot. He's brainwashed her into thinking she won't get into heaven unless she goes to his church in the city."

Nana nodded with concern.

"So what are we doing today?" I interrupted.

Nana looked at me and smiled like she had forgotten I was there. Then she snapped her fingers above her head and spun around. "*La fiesta*, remember?"

I wondered if I was going to like this party.

Mrs. Castillo added, "There'll be *música*. My son plays the guitar. His room is on the other side of the door in your room."

"Is that who I heard talking last night?" I said.

Mrs. Castillo frowned. "Did he keep you awake? I told him you were here and to be quiet."

Nana slid scrambled eggs and *chorizo* onto a plate and set it before me. "Mateo's bedroom backs up to yours. I rent the front of the house to the Castillos. I didn't want to close off the walls permanently, so we just bolt the doors closed for privacy.

"Before that, this house felt like a wide open canyon. I'm too old to be filling so many empty spaces."

I folded the eggs into a *tortilla* and pushed the spicy sausage to the side. "How old is he?"

"Thirteen," Mrs. Castillo said.

"He's a nice boy. All soap and water," Nana said.

"And good-looking too," Mrs. Castillo added with a wide grin and a wink.

"His father helps me a great deal around here." Nana said. "Don't worry, *mija*. He can't unlock the door."

The back of my neck grew warm. "Soap and water?" I could barely understand Nana's Spanish and now her English confused me.

Nana laughed. "Sweet and clean."

Mrs. Castillo wore a gold ring on every finger. She twisted each mindlessly. "Well, I better get to the beauty shop." She stood and kissed Nana on the cheek. *"Gracias por el café."* She leaned over and kissed me on the cheek too! *"Adiós."* Then she sashayed out of the room, her chubby ankles hanging over her strappy high heels.

Nana leaned against the table. "Do you want to sleep somewhere else? There are several rooms to choose from. I just thought you'd like to sleep in your mom's old room."

My mouth was stuffed with eggs and *tortilla*, so I just shook my head back and forth. The thought of packing and unpacking *again* sounded awful. I hated to admit it, but I'd never slept in such a pretty room and kind of liked it. "That room belonged to my mom?"

"Sí. You seem surprised."

"Just doesn't seem like her." I shook my head, thinking about the swirling blue walls. "Why do you think she never brought me here to visit?" I tossed my head back and stuffed the last bit of *tortilla* into my mouth before the eggs spilled out the end.

Nana turned toward the sink and began to wash the dishes. "You know how busy she is. Sometimes plans stretch so long and thin that they break and you're left with no plans at all."

She turned to me and wiped her wet hands across her apron. "But I am just pink and joy that you are here for the entire summer. I have waited a long time to get to know you and show you your culture."

"You mean tickled pink?"

"No." Nana batted her hand in the air. "Those clichés are just for unoriginal people. I use words that feel right, not sound right."

By late afternoon, I had hung star-shaped metal lanterns from the trees, set white plastic chairs against the tables, and hung a lime-colored donkey *piñata* from the twisted tree in the center of the yard. I draped multicolored cloths across the tables and lit all thirty-five votive candles at the center of each. The smell of *tamales*, *enchiladas*, and beans floated through the air. My stomach grumbled.

"Need some help?"

I spun around. A boy about my age stood in the shadows with a multicolored cloth in his hands.

"Uh, no. I think I've got it."

"You're Izzy, right?"

I folded my arms across my chest. "Yeah. Who are you?"

He grinned as he set the cloth on a nearby table. "I'm Mateo. Your nana told me and pretty much everyone else all about you."

The guy behind the wall!

Mateo stepped into the light, his toffee brown eyes dancing. "So you're from California, huh?"

"Yeah."

"What's it like there?"

I shrugged. "Sunny."

He laughed. "That's it? Just sunny?"

I didn't know what he wanted me to say. "Yeah. I guess the beach is cool. Have you ever been?"

He shook his head and a wave of dark hair fell over his left eye. "Nope. Not yet. But I plan on it someday. Is there a lot of treasure there?"

"Treasure?"

He reached up with both arms and leaned on one of the overhead branches. "Yeah, you know like legends of buried treasure and stuff."

"I've never heard of any."

"I was just wondering because I was reading this book on the West and how lots has never been found. We have treasure buried near the village. And since I'm a treasure hunter, I thought I'd check it out."

I chuckled and peered more closely at him to make sure he wasn't teasing me. "A treasure hunter?"

"Yeah. I'm gonna be an archaeologist."

"Have you ever found anything?"

"Not yet, but I will. Got the map and everything." He dropped his arms from the hanging branch, stuffed a hand into his pocket and pulled out a map.

I reached out to touch it, but he jerked his hand back. "You can't touch it."

"Why not?" I asked, twisting a loose thread on the hem of my T-shirt around my pinky.

He raised his hands and shook his head. "It's just . . . this legend. It says the map can only be touched by someone who's brave or the treasure won't be found. That's why I always carry it with me."

What made him so brave? I flipped my hair back and lifted my chin proudly. "I'm brave."

He smiled and his eyes widened. "You look brave. But I need to be sure."

Over Mateo's shoulder, I saw a tall, elegant woman approach the house carrying a plate covered by foil. She wore a white, billowy sundress that hung to her feet. She looked like a distant cloud floating across heaven. Her dark hair hung to her waist, peeking out from under a layer of white streaks, like moonbeams illuminating the midnight sky.

As she opened the back door, she turned slowly and gazed directly at me. My chest grew heavy under the weight of her intense gaze. I couldn't turn away.

"What are you staring at?" Mateo asked, turning to see.

A gentle wind moved across the yard, sweeping my hair across my eyes and blocking her from my view. I brushed it away quickly. But it was too late.

She was gone.

Mateo's voice brought me back to the moment. "That's Socorro."

"You know her?"

He laughed. "Everyone knows her. She's the village storyteller."

"Storyteller?"

"Yeah, you know. Someone who tells stories?" He tilted his head in surprise. "Don't you have those where you come from?"

I shook my head. "Are her stories good?"

"The best."

I'd never met a real storyteller.

For a moment, Mateo seemed to be measuring me up. "Tell you what. No one knows how Socorro got those white streaks in her hair. If you ask her, and she tells you, that would prove your bravery and I could show you the map."

"Why hasn't anyone ever asked her?"

Mateo leaned close, whispering, "She's a seer. She sees things no one else can, like the future. And you never ask a seer about herself."

I stepped back. "Then why would I ask her?"

He shrugged. "You're not a native villager. She'll figure you don't know the rules. And if she does tell you? You'll have discovered a huge secret." He reached out his hand. "Is it a deal?"

I broke the thread on my T-shirt hem, loosening the pressure in my pinky, and shook his hand. "It's a deal."

6

Good Heart, Solid Soul

A couple of hours later, I could hear the murmurs of a crowd gathering. I didn't want to be late and make an entrance, like I had to do on all the first days at so many new schools. I pulled on a white cotton skirt and grabbed the yellow halter top next to it. In the mirror, I noticed my bony knees popped out like swollen doorknobs.

Outside, I stood close to the house listening to laughter and music floating in the air. The whole yard smelled of Mexican spices and roses.

Searching the crowd of unfamiliar faces, I caught sight of Mateo. He sat on a stool in the corner of the yard, singing and tapping his guitar between chords. It sounded like slow,

Spanish music. Mateo's raspy voice matched the sadness of the melody and for a moment I thought I had heard the song before. Or maybe it was the sadness that was familiar.

A black wave of hair hung over his left eye and every once in a while he flashed a quick smile at the crowd. When he finished the song, he looked off to one side, nodded, and stood up.

"Hey, everyone. The Castillo *mariachi* band is almost here. You know my dad, always making an entrance."

Everyone laughed. He glanced in my direction and I quickly turned away. Was I staring?

"*Mija*, why are you just standing here alone?" Nana's small hands wrapped around my right elbow.

She led me to a shabby little woman seated alone under a swaying cottonwood near the edge of the yard. Her shoulders slumped into her chest and the lines in her face looked like the deep, worn crevices in Nana's front gate.

Nana smiled at me and her friend. "And here are my two guests of honor, Izzy and Gip."

"Happy birthday," I said.

Gip grinned up at me and then her mouth parted ever so slightly. "Ah, you have his green eyes, those unusual eyes." She pulled me closer and studied my face. "Yes, they are as light as his, as is your skin." Gip smiled. "You remind me so much of your father, dear."

I felt as though melted chocolate had oozed its way from my heart to my toes, coating me with comfort on its way down.

"I do?"

A silent look passed between Gip and Nana before Nana said, "But her spirit is all her own."

I eased into the chair next to Gip. "So you knew my dad?"

"Oh yes. Everyone knew your father. He spent many Saturdays working to help me fix up my little *adobe* home. Set the tile floors himself. And if he wasn't helping me he was helping someone else." She smiled at Nana. "He repaired half the walls in your nana's house. He could make or fix anything."

My smile reached across the universe and back.

Gip leaned forward as if she was about to say something of great importance. "He was a man of good heart and solid soul. Too good for this world of ours."

"If only I could have known him."

Nana stood up and clapped her hands. "It's *piñata* time! We should find Maggie."

"Good idea," Gip said. "Would you hand me my cane, dear?" She rolled her eyes. "That granddaughter of mine is always up to something."

I didn't want her to leave. I wanted her to tell me more about my dad. More of where I came from. I stood up and said, "I can look for her, if you want."

Gip relaxed back into her chair.

"You can't miss her. She has mounds of blonde hair, comes to about here," she tapped my ribcage, "and is six years old."

"Don't leave. I'll be right back."

As I turned to leave, she wrapped her hand around my wrist. "She won't be here at the *fiesta*. She'll be out there exploring." She nodded toward the trees beyond the grass. The same place that had swallowed my baseball the day before.

I sprinted through the rose garden and down the hill, all the while calling for a little girl I didn't even know. I ran fast, to nowhere in particular. It felt good. Just enough light remained to illuminate the path, and the evening breeze swept across my face.

Cupping my hands around my mouth, I called, "Maggie?"

I wasn't sure which direction to go next, so I stood still for a moment to catch my breath.

The wind whistled through my long hair.

Leaves rustled under light footsteps; I turned to see what was behind me.

7

THE CAT-DOG

"**H**ave you seen a little gray doggie?"

A girl with lake-blue eyes stood in front of me. The waning sunlight sliced through the trees, resting on her pale face.

"You must be Maggie."

"Hey, how do you know my name?"

"I just met Gip. She asked me to find you. I'm Izzy. I'm here with Nana for the summer."

Hesitation flashed across her squinted eyes before she smiled. "Gip told me about you."

"Really? Like what?"

She bounced up and down with the rhythm of a hiccup. "I really have to find Frida. Can you help me?"

Mariachi music drifted across the hills, reminding me I wanted to get back to Gip to talk more about my dad.

"Sure. But we need to hurry before the sun sets."

We finally found Frida stretched on her back under a tree, her gray whiskers reaching toward the sky. I had spent ten minutes looking for Frida the Dog, only to find out that Frida was a cat—a hazy gray cat with a dark patch of fur across the top of her eyes like she had one long eyebrow. Gip later told me they had named her after the famous Mexican artist, Frida Kahlo, who had the same unibrow. She even showed me a picture: "Do you see the likeness?" she'd asked.

Now, Maggie snapped a leash on Frida's collar, "Bad doggie. No puppy treats for you tonight."

"Maybe she doesn't really like puppy treats—I mean, she is a cat."

Maggie raised her finger to her lips and scowled. "Shhh. She likes being a dog. And she likes puppy treats—'specially if I pat some peanut butter all over 'em. But she won't get any peanut butter tonight."

I gave up the argument and walked with Maggie through the calm night air toward the house, surprised to see that Frida the cat-dog strolled along, happy on her leash.

"So you live with Gip?" I asked.

"Yeah." She pointed to the south. "Just a few trees and rocks that way, right above the river. Gip says it only takes an angel's wink to get there. Who do you live with?"

"My mom. In California."

"I used to live with Mommy and Daddy. But then they went to heaven."

Maggie pointed to the magenta cotton sack hanging on her back. "My mommy made this special back sack for me."

"Special?"

Maggie plopped onto the ground cross-legged and stroked Frida between the ears. "It's all knitted pretty with her yarn. She even made the coyote howling at the moon. See?" She twisted around and pointed to the yellow coyote in the middle of her back sack. "Gip told me Mommy's yarn is special and she could make just anything in this world with it. She had a basket high with bits and pieces. So, I keeped 'em and putted them in here. Sometimes I wonder if she misses her yarn. I'm going to give it back to her."

I thought about Dad's baseball and wondered if he missed it too. Then I wondered if he missed me. "How are you going to do that?"

"I'm gonna make a ladder with her yarn. All the way to heaven." Maggie looked up at me. "Do you believe in ghosts?"

"I've never seen one."

"Well I do. I seened one just last week float right out the window." She giggled. "It looked like a see-through marshmallow."

I laughed along with Maggie all the way to the edge of the lawn where the candles cast a dancing yellow light across the party.

"So how do you know it was a marshmallow if it was see through?" I asked, still chuckling.

"'Cause it smelled like one."

Maggie turned and started skipping back to the *fiesta*, with Frida trotting alongside. I followed behind, anxious to get back to Gip, and more stories about my dad.

"*Ay*, Izzy there you are. We have been waiting. *Apúrate*." Nana tugged my arm. "Come, you must break open the *piñata*. The guest of honor always takes the first swing."

Children jammed together under the cottonwood where the *piñata* swayed in the breeze as Mr. Castillo gripped the end of the rope with both hands. Nana put the bat in my hand and asked me to bend down so she could tie on the blindfold. I adjusted the red scarf around my head and was glad I couldn't see all the people watching.

Nana whirled me around slowly three times. I could feel her steady the *piñata* in front of me and place my hand on it. "It is right in front of you."

I reached my left hand out to touch the donkey, but Mr. Castillo tugged on the other end of the rope, pulling the *piñata* out of my reach.

The crowd's voices hummed softly and the cicadas buzzed in the trees. Leaning forward, I swung the bat through the air in all directions, but the *piñata* escaped me each time. Finally, I stood motionless and tried to sense where it was. Just as I was about to swing again, I felt a swoosh of air as it jerked upward. Quickly, I pulled the bat back behind my right shoulder and crashed it into the *piñata*, whacking it so hard it burst open. The crowd's murmurs became thunderous cheers. Candy clattered about my feet and everyone rushed around me.

When I removed my blindfold, children were shuffling across the grass under my feet to pick up the suckers and bubblegum. A woman in the crowd shouted, "She hits like her *papa*!"

Who said that? It felt like the crowd was spinning on a carousel and all the faces blurred together.

"Izzy, look at all my candy! You want the gum?" Maggie tugged at my arm. She had a load of candy gathered in her skirt.

"You don't like gum?" I asked.

She wrinkled her nose. "These are Chiclets from Mexico and I think they taste funny. You have to chew a whole lot to even get a wad big enough for bubbles. Then they don't blow too good of bubbles anyway."

"I'll have some. Do you know where Gip is?" I asked as I took the Chiclets from her.

"She prob'ly went home. She gets tired real easy."

"Who takes you home then?"

"I told you I only live an angel's wink away. I can walk or sometimes Mateo takes me and Frida."

A familiar voice called out, "Hey, you gonna share that gum?"

I turned around to find Mateo standing in front of me with his hands held out.

I shrugged. "Sure." I handed him a few.

"Ooh, Izzy thinks you're cute." Maggie covered her mouth and laughed.

My words got caught in my throat. I wanted to protest, but before I could even defend myself Mateo piped in.

"And where would you learn something like that?" Mateo asked with a smirk. He seemed to be enjoying himself.

"At school. If a girl thinks a boy is cute, she gives him more than one of her candy or gum or some other thing from her lunch."

"I really wasn't thinking that at all. I just gave him what was in my hand." But what I really wanted to say was I don't think he's cute and you're only six and have no idea what you're even saying. So quit bugging me!

Maggie shrugged, then ran off to something new that had caught her interest. Frida followed behind, wagging her tail like a real puppy.

Mateo stood in front of me. Close enough to see that he was a hair taller than I was. I pushed my hair behind my ears.

"So did you ask Socorro about her hair?"

"No, I never saw her again."

He nodded. "She must've left early." Mateo leaned against the tree and smiled. "I could take you to her house if you want. She lives down by the river."

"Sure." I tried to sound confident.

A loud voice called from behind me. "There you are, Mateo!" Mrs. Castillo stepped carefully across the grass, trying to avoid getting her heels stuck in the ground. She had on a strapless gold evening dress that looked more like what someone would wear to prom than a backyard party.

Mateo pushed off the tree and stood straight. "Hey, Mom."

"You need to come help clean up." She winked at me and smiled. "*Hola*, Izzy."

"Hi, Mrs. Castillo."

"No, no. It's Tía. Remember?" she said. Her hair was piled high on her head and she had little diamond barrettes fastened on top.

I nodded and smiled, "Tía."

"Isn't she *bonita*?" Tía said.

Mateo rolled his eyes. "Geez, Mom do you always have to be so embarrassing?"

The cicadas clicked and snapped their wings overhead and I suddenly wished I could grow wings and fly away.

Mateo turned to me. "I mean you *are* pretty, I guess, I mean—oh, never mind." And with that he turned and walked toward the house.

Did he really think I was pretty?

Tía laughed and rolled her eyes. "I always embarrass him. I really don't mean to. Maybe it's just because he's a teenager now. Does your mama embarrass you?"

I couldn't think of Mom ever being so forward, but wanted to make Tía feel better, so I said, "Yeah. All the time."

That night, I couldn't sleep, so I sat at the desk in my room and wrote on my story cards.

Once there was an enchanted place where people rode the skies to listen for the wind's voice. But the wind didn't talk to

*them. One day a wandering girl arrived and heard the wind call
out to her. It had a secret only she could hear.*

The steady pulse of the night was settling in and I felt the
weight of a star's heavy gaze through one of the high windows in my bedroom. I looked at the baseball, now sitting on
the little weathered desk. My bare feet felt cool against the
Saltillo tile. "What should the secret be?"

I climbed on top of the desk and slowly pressed open one
of the small overhead windows framing the stars and waited
for the wind to tell me.

Unfinished Stories
and Squished Tomatoes

"Don't you like the *calabacitas*?" Nana asked as we shared lunch the next week on the long back porch.

I stared down at my plate and scrunched up my nose. I didn't have the heart to tell her that the squash and corn was too mushy to eat.

"I guess I'm just not used to them."

"Sometimes it takes time to be comfortable with new things."

Nana stood and walked across the lawn to the vegetable garden, her bright white dress sweeping the ground. In this light, she looked like an angel. I traced my fingers over the thread of the baseball in my lap. It felt good in my hands and for some reason made me feel closer to Dad. I found myself carrying it around wherever I went.

When she returned she set two tomatoes on the table. "These you will love."

Nana sat back down and wiped the tomatoes with a napkin. She eyed the baseball in my lap. "Where did you get that?"

"I found it. It was my dad's."

Nana hesitated, her eyes searching my face. "He was a good man."

I scooted to the edge of my seat. "Tell me about him. Like what did he like to eat and where did he grow up? How did he meet my mom?"

Relaxing into her chair, Nana smiled and spoke slowly. "He grew up in Albuquerque and loved my cooking. Actually he loved anything spicy."

"Do I . . . am I like him at all?"

Nana nodded and folded her hands in her lap. "You remind me of him quite a bit. Now, try my *tomates*."

"But I want to know more about him."

Nana sliced the plumpest, largest tomato. "All stories are told in due time. Just like these needed time to grow on the vine until they were ripe." The juice slid down the back of her thumb. "An unripe story is like an unripe tomato—no good at all."

A tomato wedge slipped from Nana's grasp and fell to the ground. She handed me a fresh wedge and I popped it into my mouth. Its tangy juices spread across my tongue and down my throat. It didn't taste anything like the ones Mom bought at the grocery store.

Disappointment at another unfinished story welled up inside of me. I sighed and squished part of the tomato on the ground with my tennis shoe.

"Today I have much work to do, so I asked Mateo to take you around the village."

"I can go by myself," I said, staring down at the splattered tomato.

Nana laughed. "No, it is better to have a guide. He will take you to the center. It is the heart of the village, the people, and all of our ancestors before us." She patted me on the shoulder.

An hour later, I got tired of waiting for Mateo to show up, so I went looking for him. I zigzagged down the hillside beyond the garden. When I found him, he was asleep in a hammock tied between two cottonwood trees. I tiptoed toward the trees hoping to scare him, but instead of rolling him from the hammock like I'd planned, I stood watching his still face. For a strange moment I imagined if my father looked this peaceful when he died—then I shook the thought from my head. Stepping back, I flinched as a twig crunched beneath my feet.

Mateo jumped and pitched off the hammock onto the dirt. I covered my mouth to hide my giggles.

He stood up, brushed the dirt from the front of his jeans, and glanced toward the house. "I . . . I . . . didn't hear you. How long does it take you to eat lunch? I've been waiting an hour."

"You mean sleeping?" I mumbled. I didn't think he heard me because he clapped his hands together and said, "Ready?"

I nodded and we set off down the same narrow path I had explored on my first day at Nana's. Mateo picked up a small twig and snapped off pieces bit by bit, tossing them to the ground as we walked.

"So . . . have you always lived here?" I asked.

"My whole life." He stopped along the shaded path and raised an eyebrow. "How come you've never been here before?"

I shrugged. "My mom is working on her PhD and we've never had time, I guess."

Mateo fell in step as we continued walking. "Your mom isn't a *curandera* then?"

"A what?"

"You know, someone who heals people with herbs and stuff. People come from all over to see Nana."

"Like magic healing?"

Mateo laughed. "I dunno. I just know it works."

He nodded toward the baseball in my hand, changing the subject. "So you play?"

"I've played at school before but not on a real team or anything. Do you?"

"Only for fun."

I tossed the ball up, but before I caught it, Mateo grabbed it from midair with one hand. "What's this?" He pointed to the words scribbled across. "Looks like there's some words missing."

"I don't know. I think my dad wrote it."

He nodded like he understood.

"I figure maybe six or seven letters. And it has to be two words because you always need a subject and a verb and—"

Mateo cocked his head to one side and laughed. "What're you; like an English teacher?" He tossed the ball back to me.

I caught it with both hands. "No, but everyone knows a sentence needs a subject and a verb. At least in California they do."

He laughed—which I wasn't expecting him to do. All the boys I knew back home would've gotten mad.

"Besides I'm a writer. I should know these things," I said.

"What do you write about?"

I pitched the ball in the air and missed it coming down. Mateo jogged across the trail to pick it up.

"Whatever I think about. Like right now I'm working on a story about—" I stopped as I remembered the map. "I can't tell you. Sorry."

Mateo let that last part roll right over his shoulder and right off his back. He grinned and nodded like he remembered, too. "You should talk to Socorro about your stories." Turning the baseball in his hand, he said, "Now we just have to figure out the verb and subject. "Hey, I know a verb. Race!"

And with that he took off running down the narrow path through the trees while I followed on his heels.

He ran fast, but I could run faster. I just needed more trail. Every time I tried to pass him, he'd cut left or right, blocking me. When the path widened, I saw my chance. My lungs burned, but I called out, "Hey, Mateo!"

He threw a glance at me. I tossed the ball, just out of reach.

"Catch!"

When he slowed to catch it, I flew past him and headed for a row of brown *adobe* homes up ahead. Mateo stumbled to a stop beside me and bent over, pressing his hands to his knees and gasping between each word, "That . . . was . . . low."

I pressed a hand to my aching side and laughed. "So was calling a race without warning."

Mateo straightened, finally catching his breath, and held out the ball. "Geez. You're fast!"

I grabbed it and smiled triumphantly.

Mateo grinned back and turned down a path between two *adobe* homes. "Come on, I'll show you around."

As we passed through the village, people sat in their open courtyards, waving hello. A dog and a goat loped across the street in front of us and the same little boy who'd spilled his ice cream cone called out to them to come back.

As we crossed the road I asked, "How big is the village?"

"You're looking at it, unless you count people like us who don't live at the center. Not many people live here now; most have left for the city."

We turned left and made our way down another short block that looked the same as the one before. I imagined my dad stepping across these roads. Smiling and waving to the neighbors.

"Why do people move away?" I thought about Mom.

Mateo shrugged and grinned. "I don't know, but I'm always going to have a house here. Even when I go away to hunt treasure. I know I'll always come back. My dad says this is where our family is rooted."

I felt a pang of envy that Mateo had roots. A place to call home. Maybe that's why Mom always moved. She worried we might grow roots.

The scent of sweet bread filled the air. "How come the shops look like houses?"

Mateo tossed the baseball high into the air, and this time I caught it with one hand.

"Most of the stores are the front of someone's house."

He placed a hand on my arm, stopping me in front of a bright yellow gate with a sign above it that read *Panadería* in purple hand-painted letters. "This is my favorite one," he said with a smile.

We made our way through a small courtyard, where pink geraniums hung over the sides of terracotta pots lining the walkway. Above the bright turquoise door was a small painted tile that read *Mi casa es su casa*.

Inside, warm scents of vanilla and cinnamon floated through the air. My mouth watered while we waited. Mateo grabbed a pink box from the counter and filled it with a dozen sweet breads.

My eyes grew wide and I wondered how he could eat it all. He must've read my mind because he turned to me and said, "To take home to Nana."

Outside, Mateo handed me what looked like a *taco* sprinkled with sugar and sealed with braided edges. "It's an *empanada* with apple filling inside." He chomped his in half with one bite. His cheeks got so big I thought he'd have to spit some out just to swallow.

I took a small bite.

Mateo shook his head and swallowed. "No, no. You have to take a bigger bite to get the filling. Like this." He pulled another from the box, tossed his head back and shoved half of it in his mouth.

With one deep breath I stuffed half the *empanada* in my mouth and let the warm apple filling ooze across my tongue. It was delicious.

Mateo laughed. "See? It's good, huh?"

I nodded and smiled as best I could with my full mouth.

We passed a florist, a grocer, and several fruit stands. People strode through the village and smiled as we walked by. An old man with a walking stick tipped his straw hat and said, "*Buenos días*, Mateo." By the time we reached the center square of the village I had polished off three *empanadas*.

"That's the village church," Mateo pointed toward the same church I had passed with Mr. Castillo.

The church stood at the east end, marking what Mateo said was the border of the village. More store fronts faced the plaza, where a blanket of green grew beneath a cluster of large cottonwood trees. We plopped onto the grass to cool off in the shade. I rolled the baseball across the grass to Mateo.

He leaned on his elbows and squinted into the sun streaming through the trees and stared at the ball closely. "So, do you believe in magic?" he rolled the ball back to me.

The grass felt cool beneath my hands. "What kind of magic? Like wishes and stuff?"

"Nah, more like stuff you can't explain any other way. Like the way Socorro can see the future. Hey—" Mateo was distracted by something behind me. "Speaking of . . . look." Mateo snapped upright.

I turned to where Mateo pointed. There in the distance Socorro glided up the stone steps into the church. "She looks pretty busy."

I didn't feel ready to talk to Socorro. Not about her hair and for sure not about my stories.

"Well, then let's wait for her," he said.

I felt trapped. If I said no, Mateo would think I wasn't brave. I stood up and brushed the grass off my shorts. "I can't."

Mateo jumped up. "Why?"

Looking at my watch I sputtered, "I gotta go. My mom might call tonight." It wasn't a complete lie. She had said she'd try and call whenever she was near a phone. But she hadn't called. What if she never did? What if the summer was forever? I remembered her words the night she spoke to Nana back in California: *Do you think she'll forgive me?*

Mateo sighed. "Oh, well when do you want to go see her?"

I put my hands on my hips. "You don't believe she's going to call."

"I didn't say that." He stepped back in surprise. "Why would you think that?"

"Well, she is. Tonight!" I scooped my ball from the grass and squeezed it until my knuckles turned white.

Mateo rested his hand on my shoulder. "Hey, are you okay?"

"You don't even know me and I don't want to go on your dumb treasure hunt!" I whipped around to make my way back to Nana's.

Mateo followed on my heels. "Hey, wait up! I was just saying that maybe it's a sign that Socorro showed up." He lagged. "And my treasure hunt isn't dumb!"

I left Mateo behind and ran back to Nana's. I didn't need him to like me. And what was so great about his treasure hunt anyway? I gripped the baseball. Why hadn't Mom called?

A small breeze curled around my arm, urging me away from the path toward the river.

Bella, it said with a whisper.

"You have the wrong girl. My name is Izzy!"

Nana's house glowed in the distance, and I pulled away from the wind before it passed overhead.

9

TORTILLAS ARE LIKE LIFE

The postcard arrived two days later. The picture on the front showed a waterfall swallowed up by the green jungle. A bright green-and-orange bird floated in the sky.

Dear Izzy,

The rain forest is amazing. I saw a baby croc and a spider monkey this morning. The quetzal birds are incredibly bright. They have bright green heads and crimson bodies (like the one on the front). Sometimes they look like they are suspended on strings in the sky. Did you see the full moon on Sunday night?

Love, Mom

It was strange and kind of comforting to think that even though Mom was far away we shared the same sun, moon, and stars. It surprised me she noticed the moon though. She was always too busy to pay attention to that sort of thing. One time, the moon was so fat and big I thought I could reach out and touch it from our apartment balcony. I called to Mom to come and see, but she just nodded with her face in a book and said, "Yes, isn't it pretty?"

I traced my fingers over the picture of the waterfall. Why hadn't she called? Didn't she miss me at all? I had so much to tell her.

I sat at the desk to write her a letter.

Dear Mom,

I got your postcard and even though I can't mail this to you, it makes me feel like I am talking to you. Are you having fun? Sometimes the wind talks to me. It wants me to follow it. What do you think it wants to tell me?

Beyond the high windows in the distance, a bright yellow hot air balloon floated by, tiny as a bumblebee.

"Izzy?" Nana called from the kitchen.

I stuffed the letter in the drawer and hurried toward the kitchen for my first *tortilla*-making lesson.

As I dashed around the corner toward the kitchen, I slammed my forehead right into the top of the doorframe. *Wham!* I rubbed my aching head. Nana's hundred-year-old house had narrow, short doorways designed to slow enemy attacks during times of war. Plus it helped hold the heat and cool in, but I liked the battle reason better.

Nana laughed. "I can always hear you coming, Izzy. When will you learn to slow down and duck?"

The doorways sure would've been great protection against tall enemies. But Nana, with her four-foot-eleven-inch frame, had no problems walking through them, while I had a throbbing head.

In the kitchen, sunlight bounced across the walls, and the soothing scent of cranberry and lavender filled the air. Just walking into this room made me feel good, like lying in the warm sun and squishing my toes into soft sand.

"Are you ready, *mija?*"

"Yep."

"Then wash your hands and make sure to say the Hail Mary *tres* times to get all the germs off."

Suddenly, my throat throbbed like I'd swallowed a baseball. "But I don't know it."

Nana raised an eyebrow. "You don't know the Hail Mary? Didn't your mama ever take you to church?"

I shook my head, feeling small and stupid.

She took a deep breath. "We can say it together." As I washed, Nana recited the words, "Hail Mary, full of grace..."

By the third time, I had memorized the last bit of the prayer. *Pray for us sinners now and at the hour of our death.*

Nana wrapped a worn yellow apron around my waist and gave me a squeeze.

"Now, first thing to know is that *tortilla* making is a lost art, but you don't ever want to buy *tortillas* from the store, *mija*," she said. "They taste like rubber."

Nana pinned her hair up on her head with a pencil. "And the second thing is that *tortillas* are like life. It is best to keep it simple. For *tortillas* we need only white flour, lard, and hot water."

I sat on a lopsided wooden stool at the edge of the counter and watched her small, robust hands mix the ingredients. She prepared two separate bowls, one for each of us.

"Did you ever teach Mom to do this?" I asked.

Nana nodded. "I tried. Now put your hands into the bowl and knead the dough."

I pushed, pulled, twisted, and squeezed. But my dough didn't look anything like Nana's. It felt warm and gooey and stuck to my hands like glue. "I don't think this is right."

Nana chuckled and set my bowl aside, then handed me her own. "Your mama never liked cooking. She always preferred being outdoors. Here. Knead this dough."

I wiped my sticky fingers across my apron and tried again. I pinched the dough between my fingers.

"Ah, *mijita.* It's not Play-Doh! Do not press so hard. Be more delicate. Just let it take shape."

"Maybe I'm not meant to make *tortillas.*"

"You can do anything you set your heart to." We started again, but this time she helped me. She pressed my hands into the dough. Her hands felt like smooth pieces of glass.

"*Tortilla* making seems hard at first—it's no bowl of *sopaipillas,* but keep at it and you will be a master *tortilla* maker in no time at all." Nana smiled and pointed to the bowl. "*Mira,* no stickies. Let's get Martha now."

"Who's Martha?"

Nana raised her eyebrows like I should know this. "She is one of the patron saints of cooks." She took the plastic St. Martha statue from the windowsill and sat her next to the bowl. She stood maybe three inches high. One hand was placed over her chest and the other carried a cross. Then, Nana reached into a small cabinet, removed an amber spice bottle, and sprinkled something over the dough.

"This is a very special recipe. *La sagrada.* And this is the secret ingredient. People from all over Albuquerque come for these *tortillas.* It gets so I can't keep up at times.

But I only use the secret ingredient when someone really needs it."

"Like when would they need it?"

"Well, Maggie likes to eat them when Gip is extra pale and she is worried. Mrs. Gomez next door ate so many when her husband died that now she looks like a stuffed *taco*." Nana folded in the secret ingredient with her hands. "And sometimes it has nothing to do with sadness. Maybe someone's heart just needs a blessing."

"Do you know when someone needs it because you're a *cura*?" I asked.

She laughed. "You mean *curandera*?"

"Yeah, that."

She sprinkled flour onto the pine table and made balls from the dough. I pinched off a piece and copied her motions. "*Muy bien,* Izzy. Slowly. Patiently."

Next, she pressed her wooden rolling pin into one of the balls, turning and flattening it. "Oh, *mija*, you are full of such good questions. *Sí,* I am a *curandera*. I know the old ways of finding and blending herbs to ease pain and heal others. Who told you that?"

"Mateo."

"Ah. So you two are friends?"

I hoped so, but wasn't sure what he thought of me after the way I had freaked out.

"I guess. So what kind of sickness? Like stomachaches?" I rolled my lopsided little ball with the rolling pin, but it didn't become round like Nana's. The misshapen dough looked more like the state of Texas. "Mine doesn't look like yours."

Nana smiled and kept working. "Just be patient. Try again."

She told me all the sickness she cured, like stomachaches, headaches, rashes, allergies—those sorts of things.

"What about a broken heart? Can you cure that?" I pushed the rolling pin against the dough hard and quick, thinking about Mom.

Nana stopped pressing and wiped her hands across the front of her apron. "The *tortillas* can open the heart a little at a time, to let out the sadness or fill up the emptiness. But only if the person is ready."

"How do you know if you're ready?"

Nana raised her fist over her chest. "You know in here, like something is missing."

"Like how I feel about my dad? And how it's worse because Mom never wants to talk about him?"

Nana nodded and squinted like she was thinking hard about this. Soft wrinkles formed around her eyes. "*Sí, mija.*"

I waited for her to shut me down, like Mom, but she nodded like it was all right for me to keep going. I took a deep breath and let it out slowly. "The other night at the *fiesta*, someone said 'she hits like her *papa*.' What did that mean?"

Nana motioned toward the uncooked *tortillas*. "Hand me those so I can put them on the *comal*." I stood up and handed them to her one at a time as she snapped them on and off the flat, iron pan with the speed of a frog's tongue catching its prey. I knew I'd never be as fast as Nana.

She stacked the *tortillas* in a basket. Before they even cooled, I grabbed one off the top and slathered butter all over it, then drizzled honey in the center and rolled it tight.

We sat at the long table in the kitchen and enjoyed our hard work. The first bite tasted warm and earthy. It eased its way into my stomach and filled me up.

Nana swiped her pinky across a dot of honey on the table. "It's only natural for a girl to want to know her father."

I pulled another *tortilla* from the basket on the table and drizzled it with honey.

"Your mama was very young when she met him." Nana sighed. "I didn't approve of him at first."

"Why not?" I asked.

"Oh, I always dreamed she would marry a Hispanic Catholic like me and my mama and hers before that." She looked up at me through a lock of salt-and-pepper hair that had fallen from her bun. "Gip was right, you look a lot like him."

"I do?" The sweet honey coated my insides.

"Yes, you have his cheekbones." She moved my hair from my face. "And his eyes, *exactamente*. He was very handsome, your father," she continued.

"Why won't Mom talk about him?"

"She only wants to protect you, *mija*."

"From what?"

"From pain I suppose. She has always avoided pain—even as a little girl."

I raised my eyebrows, puzzled.

"When she was very young she used to rush down to the river to look for fishermen. She would hide in the bushes for just the right moment. And when the fishermen put the fish in their baskets, she would sneak up and take the fish." She laughed. "Then she would run downstream and release them! Oh, how she cried for the ones she couldn't save."

"Really?" I laughed too. "That doesn't even sound like her."

Nana nodded. "Well, sometimes people change and ignore their essence."

"Essence?"

"It's what you are born to be. For me? I was born to be a *curandera*. And you will have your own path. Does that make sense?"

"Sort of."

"Now, back to your good question. Your mama and papa met when they were just sixteen. He was a star of the high school baseball team. Your papa could smack a ball to the stars."

Nana slathered a square of melting butter into a *tortilla* and continued. "They fell in love quickly, as many young lovers do, and married during their first year of college."

I stuffed the last bit of *tortilla* into my mouth and licked the dripping honey off my fingers.

"Soon after their marriage she became pregnant with you."

Nana's words echoed across the sun-washed walls and filled my empty spaces like I had eaten ten *tortillas*.

"The whole village celebrated. Everyone was so eager for you to come," she said.

"Really?"

"Of course. You were to be the daughter and grand-daughter of healers."

"My mom is a healer?"

"She is a natural. But she has chosen not to practice her gift. You see, I was trained in the ways, but your mama, she didn't even need the training. She could go out in the moonlight with her eyes closed to pick a healing flower. She needed only her instincts. It was like magic."

Nana glanced at the clock on the wall. "That is all for today. I am late for cards with Gip and Tía. Remember, some stories need to be unfolded slowly so we can appreciate what's inside of them."

"But what do you mean by magic?"

Nana carried the basket to the kitchen counter and set it down. "It means something is enchanting and special. You being here is magic. A hummingbird's wings, the buzzing bee, the way the sun rises every day no matter what. That's magic." A warm breeze drifted in through an open window carrying the scent of Nana's roses just outside. She closed her eyes and smiled. "And sometimes you can't see the magic, you just know it's there because you can feel it."

She opened her eyes and turned to me. "Life is magic."

Nana's words floated through the air to me on the tips of the breeze. And then I remembered the missing words on the baseball.

As soon as Nana left, I ran to Estrella and picked up the baseball from the nightstand, tracing my fingers over it carefully. "Because life is magic?" I whispered. "Is that what you wrote,

Dad?" The words fit, but somehow didn't feel right. The way Nana described it, anything and everything could be magic. That made figuring out the missing words so much harder.

Sinking into the chair, I thought about everything Nana had told me about my dad, especially how he could hit a ball to the stars. I pulled out a story card and a pen.

One summer night a handsome prince asked the girl he loved which star she liked best. She pointed to the brightest one in the sky. But the next night it had disappeared. So he set off on a journey in search of her favorite star to bring it back and . . . How would he bring back a star? He'd have to reach heaven.

Tapping the baseball with the pen I wondered how someone might reach heaven? A mountain top? An airplane? I traced my finger across the empty space between the words *because* and *magic.*

"Just two little missing words," I whispered.

The missing words reminded me of Mrs. Barney, who'd given me the story cards. She said that stories are made up of many pieces. She'd explained: "Letters are the pieces strung together to make a word. Words make sentences. And sentences make stories. It's piece by piece. Do you get it?"

I kind of got it, but wasn't completely sure. I didn't want her to think she'd wasted her time on me so I just nodded and whispered, "Piece by piece."

10

THE GHOST TRAIL

The next day, I made a beeline for the hammock. Dangling my right leg over the side, the hammock swayed back and forth beneath the trees as I tossed Dad's baseball into the air. My bare toes curled into the soft earth.

"Hey, Izzy."

I snapped straight up when I saw Mateo standing over me. "Hi."

Silence surrounded us like the shadows beneath the trees.

Mateo leaned against a long walking stick he was carrying. "I was wondering, if . . . do you . . ." He pushed the end of the stick into the ground. "I'm going to the ghost trail today."

I swung my leg over the hammock and stood up. "Ghost trail?" I said, glad he was still talking to me after I'd run away yesterday.

"Just a place haunted by spirits." He stood a little straighter. "If you're not busy, maybe you can come along."

"I'm not busy," I said trying to sound casual. I didn't want to sound like a chicken and ditch him again.

"So you want to go?" His voice rose with excitement.

"Sure." I plunked down onto the ground to put on my socks and tennis shoes. As I looped the laces, I said, "Hey, I'm sorry I acted like . . . I don't usually—"

"Acted like what?" Mateo sat down next to me. The afternoon sunlight danced across his chocolate eyes.

I breathed a sigh of relief and smiled. Mateo helped me to my feet and I reached back into the hammock for the baseball before we zigzagged down the trail. It wasn't long before the wind rolled gently across the landscape, a soft breath caressing my back and swishing in my ears.

Come.

I slowed my pace and turned toward the wind carefully, afraid I might disturb its whisper. But when I thought I heard it echoing from the north, it switched directions and flowed south. I got so frustrated I finally stopped and shouted, "Where?"

Mateo spun around, like he'd already seen a ghost.

"Sorry, I just—"

"You just what? Gave me a heart attack?"

Mateo must've thought I was the strangest girl in the universe. "I didn't mean to, I just thought I heard something. Didn't you hear it?"

"Hear what?"

I popped a sour ball into my mouth. "Want one?"

"No. But I wanna hear what you think you heard," Mateo said.

Now I just felt stupid for saying anything at all. I rolled the sour ball to the side of my mouth. "Ever since I got here, to Nana's house, I keep thinking I hear the wind whisper, 'Come.'"

"So why don't you follow it?"

Mateo had a way of always saying the right thing. I pushed my bangs out of my eyes. "How do you follow the wind?"

He leaned against his walking stick. "Just listen to the direction it's coming from, then you'll see where it goes and you can follow it. If it ends up being nothing then you'll know you're just *loca*." He laughed and turned back up the twisted shady trail. "You are an unusual girl, Izzy Roybal."

Was that a good thing? I swallowed the last traces of the sour ball.

"There it is." Mateo pointed with his stick. A winding trail, lined with dead twisted trees with black straggled limbs, looped up a hill and out of sight.

"Off over there, a huge fire came through 'bout a hundred years ago. The trees still haven't grown back. Weird, huh?

"The legend says that a group of *caballeros* came through here looking for the treasure. And this is where they were last seen. But their bodies and horses were never found." Mateo turned toward the trail. "Let's check it out."

"Really? Is it safe to go up there?" I asked.

Mateo continued. "I've never gone past the top of the hill. No one has that I know of. Legend has it that if you climb down the other side, your eyeballs will burn right out of your head."

"Then why are you going?" I asked.

Mateo shrugged and turned toward the haunted trail. "Maybe I'll run into a ghost who knows where to find the treasure."

I had no intention of running into a ghost on some haunted trail. "You should go first and then holler to let me know if you make it. I'll watch this end of the trail."

Mateo laughed. "Fine, I'll go alone."

After he left me standing alone, the sun peeked through the branches overhead, casting long ribbonlike shadows on the ground.

I tossed the ball into the air and caught it just as a mild breeze glided through my hair, soft like Mom's hands and Nana's voice. I turned to meet the warm air now tickling my hands, pulling me away from the haunted trail. A light familiar voice floated through the trees.

Bella.

I raised one hand in the air, trying to grab hold of the swishing wind as I thought about Nana's words: *Sometimes you can't see the magic; you just know it's there because you can feel it.*

Just as I felt the breeze take hold of my hand, Mateo came tearing down the path screaming and holding his eyes. Blood flowed down his face.

"Aaahh!" I screamed just as he ran right into me and knocked me to the ground. It wasn't until my left elbow hit earth with a bang that I heard him laughing.

Mateo's weight pushed against me. I tried to roll out from under him but we got all tangled up, and before I knew it his grinning face was two inches from mine. His dark eyes danced with amusement.

"I can't believe you! I thought you were actually hurt. And you butted in just as I was going to follow the wind."

Still laughing, Mateo raised a hand to apologize. I pushed him away and stood up. I laughed a little too, not because I thought his stupid prank was funny but because he looked like one big cherry mess with all the red face paint streaked across his cheeks.

"It's not funny," I said.

"Oh, come on. Where's your sense of humor?"

I turned on my heels and marched toward Nana's, picking up my baseball on the way. Mateo tried to walk next to me. As soon as his stride matched mine, I raced ahead.

"Izzy, come on. It was just a joke. I said I was sorry."

He tugged at my elbow. "Could you slow down for one sec?"

"Why?"

"So I can talk to you and see your face. I can't tell if you're kidding or not."

I stopped and turned to glare at him.

"Okay, so you're not kidding. Just one nod of forgiveness?" Then he smiled and clasped his hands together, raising them to his face in a pleading kind of way.

I folded my arms across my chest, still glaring. "I felt the wind, but then you showed up, and now—"

"I said I was sorry."

It was useless to try and keep my smile inside. I cracked a small grin and gave one curt nod. "I'll forgive you on one condition."

"What? Anything."

"I can't tell you now. I get to save it, like a lucky penny. And when I need a favor you have to promise to do what I ask."

"Fine," he mumbled. "I'm sorry I made you miss the wind."

"It's fine. I just have to make sure to follow it faster next time."

"Or you can go looking for it."

"How?" I asked.

He smiled and draped his arm over my shoulder. "Where it blows strongest."

Then he pointed to the sky.

11

THE BALLOON
IN THE CHURCH

The following afternoon was unusually cool and crisp. I leaned into the lounge chair, gazing at the pink glow hugging the treetops in the distance. I listened for the wind, but the air was still and silent.

Nana's story about my parents stirred inside me. Knowing just a few details about my dad, how he played baseball and loved Mom, made me feel connected to him.

Across the courtyard, Mr. Castillo slowly pushed the gate open.

"Izzy, I wasn't expecting you." He tipped his hat back. "I hope I didn't startle you."

I smiled. "No. I was just thinking."

He turned off the electric switch by the French doors. "I came by to check the pump on the fountain. Your nana says it isn't working." After pulling off the top tier of the fountain, he stuck his arm inside.

"Are you having a good time this summer?" he asked.

"Yeah, it's really different from California." Mr. Castillo seemed like the happiest and simplest person I'd ever met. It was easy being around him. I felt a tug of envy that Mateo had him for a father.

Mr. Castillo pulled a small black box from the fountain and held it up to the sky for inspection. His eyes shone like polished black stones.

"Oh, *sí*. The village is different from anywhere on Earth, I think. Perfect skies, perfect wind."

The memory of our first visit in the truck flashed in my mind. *People come from all over to ride these skies.*

The wind would be stronger up high, like Mateo had said. I leapt from the chair. "Remember when you told me the village has a hot air balloon?"

He nodded.

"Do you think we could find it?"

He fiddled with the little black box and laughed. "You know, it got me thinking that day I met you how long it's been since I rode the skies myself. I finally remembered where the balloon was stored." He set the box back in the fountain and replaced the top. "I think it's in the old chapel behind the church."

I wrapped my arms around my waist to keep from quivering. "Could I see it?"

Mr. Castillo flipped the switch near the French doors and the water flowed from the top of the fountain, splashing over the sides. "Just needed to be cleared out is all." Mr. Castillo smiled. "Can you go now?"

"Yes," I said excitedly.

"We'd better head over before the sun sets. There isn't any electricity out there."

I hurried behind him out the gate.

Mr. Castillo parked his truck in back of the church and we walked together toward the chapel, crisscrossing down the rocky hill.

"This used to be the village church before the new one was built. Must be a hundred years old."

A smaller version of the *adobe* church stood in a thicket of trees. Long fissures ran down the walls like cracks in the sun-dried ground after a rainstorm. Strands of straw poked out from the exposed *adobe* bricks.

"We didn't have the heart to tear it down, so we use it for storage." Mr. Castillo pushed open the dilapidated door, just barely hanging on its hinges, and we stepped inside.

The air was thick and musty. We zigzagged through piles of boxes, dusty toys, broken chairs, even an old doghouse. Each item or box was labeled with family names: Sanchez, Garcia, Solis. Toward the back of the shed was a tall stack of more boxes. We followed the streams of sunlight filtering through the small stained-glass window, bathing the dark corner in pink light.

"There it is," Mr. Castillo said, like he'd found a long lost friend.

Specks of dust swirled in the sunlight above a huge basket that nearly came to my shoulder. I traced my fingers over the intricate weave. A strip of dark brown wicker poked out from the side.

"This is it. I'm going to fly the skies, to talk to the wind," I whispered as I tucked the loose wicker strip back into place.

"You want to climb inside?" Mr. Castillo asked.

I nodded eagerly.

He lifted me into the basket.

"Hey, there's some stuff in here." I bent down to sift through a jacket, an old pair of shoes, and a white jersey. I held the jersey up to the early evening light. "What's this?" I asked.

Mr. Castillo stepped back and cleared his throat. "I didn't know anything was still in here."

I glanced down at the jersey in my hands, and saw the name Reed stitched on the back.

"Was this my dad's?"

Mr. Castillo nodded. "We flew together all the time."

All this belonged to my dad? I turned the jersey around. Across the front, black letters trimmed in yellow read *Pirates*.

Mr. Castillo spoke softly. "He played in the pros."

I pressed it against my body. "Dad was a professional baseball player?" I said, barely above a whisper. "Was he famous?"

"A star on the rise. You should've seen him smack a ball across center field." Mr. Castillo swung an imaginary bat and gazed toward the stained-glass window.

I shook the dust from the jersey and held it to my face, breathing it in.

Still gazing out the window he said, "It was hard on all of us when he drowned in the river. But he saved your mama. If only I had been there that day. . . ."

"Drowned? To save Mom?" I jumped over the edge of the basket, knocking over a stack of boxes nearby.

Mr. Castillo looked back at me suddenly and rubbed the back of his neck. His black almond eyes drooped with sadness. "Didn't you . . . I thought . . . I'm sorry. You need to talk to your nana."

Tears trembled in the corners of my eyes making everything blurry. I was tired of no one telling me the whole truth. I darted from the shed into the twilight.

"Izzy, wait! Let me drive you." Mr. Castillo called after me.

Darkness was fast approaching, but I didn't care. My feet hammered the earth. I sprinted past the church, through the plaza, and down the hills behind the *adobes*.

Why hadn't Mom told me the truth?

The words echoed in my head all the way to Nana's house. I gripped my dad's jersey tighter as I made my way past the rose garden. When I reached the house, breathless, I threw open the back door, and shouted for Nana.

I found her in the living room folding towels. "Why didn't you tell me?" I held up the jersey. "He drowned? Saving Mom?"

Nana stood up. A look of acceptance crossed her face. Had she known I would find his things? Was she only waiting for me to discover the missing pieces?

"Please, Izzy. Sit with me."

I didn't move.

"Please." She motioned toward the sofa. I sat down next to her, clutching Dad's jersey on my lap.

She traced over the hem of the jersey. "He was just twenty years old when the Pittsburgh Pirates recruited him. He'd only been in college for two years."

A thousand fireworks went off in my head at once. Nana's eyes glanced around the room as if she were looking for the right words. Then she turned to me and spoke slowly.

"Let me start at the beginning." She smoothed her hand over the top of mine. "Your papa loved our culture and my cooking. He learned Spanish and wanted to build a house here in the village." Nana shook her head. "Your mama got so mad when the doctors told her she couldn't move with him to Pittsburgh after he'd been recruited. But he just traveled back and forth and said this was the best place on Earth to live."

I released Nana's hand. "Why couldn't she move?"

"She had a few complications during the pregnancy and needed to stay in the care of her doctor in Albuquerque."

"So Mom just lived here in the village while he was away?"

"Well, she didn't want to. But she stayed here because your papa wanted her to be close to me and the doctor just in case."

Suddenly I realized that if Dad had saved Mom that meant she had to have already been pregnant. Which meant he'd saved me too. I gripped the jersey tighter. "What happened?"

"Well you were a fussy baby even in your mama's tummy and this worried your mother." Nana glanced toward the burning candle on Mary's altar across the room. Cranberry scents filled the air. "Your mama found a doctor in Albuquerque who specialized in these kinds of things." Nana's eyes drifted toward the stream of moonlight bathing the *Saltillo* floor, as if she could still see the moments in time she was describing.

"Keep going."

"Your parents were picnicking on the Rio Grande. It was an unusually hot spring day. The wind was strong enough to push angels from clouds."

She took a deep breath. "Your mama waded in, just to cool off her feet, but she must have lost her balance, because she fell in and the rush of the water pushed her down. Of course your father jumped in to save her. The river was so high that year, like it is now." She shook her head.

"He pushed your mom toward a log in the river where she grabbed hold, but when she looked back, your papa was nowhere to be seen. His leg had become wedged between two rocks." Nana wiped a tear from her cheek. "She was eight months pregnant."

My head started to spin in circles, making me dizzy.

And like the wind, Nana warmly touched my cheek. "I'm sorry. This is so much to hear at once."

I pulled the jersey over my head and wrapped my arms around myself. It smelled of fresh earth after a summer rain. I ran my hands down the front, smoothing the worn lines. "Don't stop."

"When your mother was brought to shore, the shock of it all sent her into labor. Thank goodness other people were with her. And that's where you were born, *mija.*"

"I was born on the river?"

"*Sí.* You came out so quickly that no one had time to get your mother to the hospital." She took my hand in hers. "But you, you were the *milagro*, the miracle, Izzy. You were born early, but strong."

"Mom said he died before I was born." My voice quivered.

"Your mother thought it was a bad omen to have a birth and death on the same day. She was just trying to protect you."

I pictured a calendar in my head and put an *X* over my birthday. No wonder she always seemed so unhappy on my birthday.

"It's my fault," I said. "He died saving me. Maybe I wasn't meant to be born."

Nana squeezed my hand. "No! When it is our time to go, it is our time and nothing can stop that. And when it is our time to be born, we come to this earth. Don't you ever think it was your fault." She tilted my chin upward to make eye contact. "Do you hear me?" she whispered. "We weren't made to understand the ways of the Lord, but we have to trust that everything happens for a reason."

"Why didn't Mom give me his last name?"

Nana straightened the stack of towels on the coffee table. "You are just as much Reed as you are Roybal. Your mama went back to her maiden name after . . . to get a fresh start, I suppose." She hesitated for a moment and just as she opened her mouth to say more, the phone rang.

Nana scooted to the edge of the sofa to stand.

"Don't answer it. I want to hear the rest of the story."

"It might be important."

"Please."

Nana and I looked at each other for what seemed like forever waiting for that dumb phone to stop ringing. I knew it would be quicker just to answer it than to let it ring.

Finally, I sprang from the sofa impatiently and ran to the phone. Dad's jersey hung almost to my knees. "Hello?"

"Izzy?"

"Mom?"

"I've been calling and calling, but couldn't get through. How are you? How's the village?" She took a deep breath and laughed. "I have so much to tell you. It's—"

Static filled the long distance between us.

"Can you hear me, Izzy?" Her voice crackled.

"Mom? Wait." I moved the phone to my other ear. "Why didn't you tell me about Dad?"

"Dad?" The next words were garbled before she said, "Did you hear me?"

"No. You're breaking up." I tapped the phone with my fingers before placing it back against my ear. "Mom, I need to talk to you."

Three seconds of clear reception followed, long enough for Mom to say, "I love you."

Before I could say another word, the phone went dead.

12

THE SECRET INGREDIENT

"Izzy, wake up," Nana whispered as she shook me by the shoulders the next night.

I rubbed my eyes and sat up. "What time is it?"

"It's midnight. There is no time to lose. Hurry, get dressed."

I threw on some clothes, half-dazed, then I followed her out the house. "But where are we going?"

"To the mesa above the river. Tonight we are gathering *yerbas*. Come, come."

Outside, the cool air cut through my sleepiness. The flashlight lit the path in front of us. I followed close as Nana led me down the trail toward the other side of the river.

At the water's edge the currents tumbled past in a sea of white that reflected the light of the moon. With each step I thought about my dad. Did it hurt to drown? Had he been afraid?

Nana and I crossed the swaying bridge held together loosely by wood planks and rope.

She gripped my hand. "Be careful where you step. This bridge is very old and sometimes moves so much I think it might throw me over."

We reached the top of a cliff that overlooked the valley below. By the moonlight, the life beyond the river stood still. The quiet ached for attention.

"What's a *yerba*?"

"Herbs. And they must be picked at the right time. There are cycles I must respect, like the lunar cycle."

We hiked along the edge of the cliff, and even though I didn't completely understand what we were doing, I felt part of something. Kind of like being picked first for a team at school. Nana's head moved back and forth as she surveyed the land in front of her. She crouched over the ground and picked up handfuls of dirt, sifting each through her small fingers.

"Ah, yes, here it is." Nana dropped down onto her knees. "Come take a closer look."

I got down on all fours and pushed my face close to the ground. "I don't see anything."

"Here. Shine the light over here." She pointed to a small three-leafed plant barely sticking out of the earth.

"See?" she whispered.

"Why are we whispering?"

"We don't want to wake the village, *mija*."

"No one can hear us up here."

She raised her left eyebrow. "Oh, *sí*. The sounds of this valley carry for miles. I can hear even the smallest bird calling across this river from the *casa*."

She pointed again at the plant. "This is a medicinal plant and it is very powerful. It is the most potent at night and can only be plucked from the earth under the light of the moon. It won't have the same power if it is picked tomorrow. Timing is the most important thing."

She removed a small velvet pouch from her waist and gently tugged on the plant. "When you pull the *yerba* from its home, you must always leave some of the root behind, so the plant has a place to heal and grow."

The moonlight cast a soft shadow across half of Nana's smooth round face and for a moment I got a glimpse of what she might have looked like when she was young.

"What does it do?" I asked.

Nana smiled. "This *yerba* is one of the most special because it can only be picked once every twelve months. But a little goes a long way. This is part of what goes into my *tortillas*. It is a secret my own nana shared with me."

Beyond the village, the Albuquerque lights flickered like a thousand tiny twinkling stars. A distant howl flew on the edge of an approaching wind; within seconds it had found us on the mesa. It whipped around, loosening Nana's bun and then descended into the village below, gliding like a ghost.

13

SOME THREADS ARE SHORTER THAN OTHERS

The next morning Nana stood on the back portal beating dust from a rug while I watered the potted flowers. Just as I turned off the hose, Frida dashed across the lawn toward me, meowing loudly. Looping and winding through my legs, she whimpered as I crouched down and scratched under her chin.

"What is it, girl? Where's Maggie?"

Without a word, Nana gathered up her skirt and scampered across the lawn. I followed behind her down the hillside. I didn't need to ask where we were going.

When we arrived at Gip's little *adobe* home, Gip was on the bumpy tile floor; she lay very still. Maggie sat on a tattered rug next to her, stroking her hair and whispering, "I'm here, Gip."

"What happened?" Nana asked as she rushed to Gip's side.

"Gip looked tired. Maybe that's why she fell on the coffee table." Maggie rubbed the tears off her pink cheeks. "I knew you'd come."

"I'm fine. Just help me up," Gip said.

Nana waved me over. "Izzy, help me move her to the sofa."

I reached under Gip's left arm while Nana lifted Gip's right. "Careful Izzy; we must be gentle. Does it hurt, Gip? Tell us if it hurts."

Gip shook her head. "No, no. Just get me to the sofa so I can rest."

"Lay her gently," Nana said.

"Do you need a pillow or anything?" I asked.

Gip smiled and closed her eyes, "No, dear. This is fine."

The left side of Gip's thin face had a long gash and her left eye was beginning to swell like a water balloon. I turned away from the blood and saw Maggie sitting on the floor.

I walked over and knelt down. "Hey, Maggie. I think she'll be all right." As soon as I said those words, I wished I could take them back. What if she wasn't?

Maggie held up four fingers. "Last time I stayed with your nana for four days."

"Last time?"

She nodded. "Gip has to get help lots."

Once we'd settled Gip on the couch with a cool cloth over her eye, Nana walked me out to the porch. Tears collected like little pools in her eyes.

"Is she going to be okay?" I asked, hoping I wouldn't be a liar to Maggie.

Despite the tears, Nana's voice remained steady and calm. "I need you to take care of Maggie while I go with Gip."

"Go where?"

"Back to the hospital. She needs her doctor."

My head felt fuzzy. "What do you mean? Can't you help her?"

Nana shook her head. "She needs more than I can give. I will explain later. Just take Maggie and Frida home with you."

"We'll go right now."

"Good. Give her a snack and try to distract her. I'll call you in an hour or so."

I turned to go inside for Maggie when Nana grabbed hold of my arm. "Please light the Santa Ana and Mary candles when you get back to the house."

Nana had said an hour, but that hour grew fat and round until it felt like it would explode. Each second ticked by at the pace of Earth rotating around the sun. Outside, the trees bent to the wind's command. I wanted to run with it all the way to Costa Rica. Or to anywhere that death and sickness couldn't climb the walls and come inside.

"You wanna play a game?" Maggie asked as she stroked Frida gently on her lap.

"You know how to play Go Fish?" I asked.

"Yeah. I know where the cards are." She set Frida down and ran to the kitchen. She returned with a deck of cards with little cherubs' faces on the backs.

We sat on the floor around the coffee table in the living room. Maggie scattered the cards on the table and pushed them back into a neat pile.

"Hey, Maggie, why do you call her Gip?"

"When I was really little I couldn't say grandma, so I put grandma and her name, Pauline, together to make 'Gip.' Sounds better, don't you think?"

I nodded.

"You deal," I said.

Maggie was intent, dealing out the cards one by one, but her shoulders, slumping into her chest, and her arms hanging like limp spaghetti noodles made her look small and hollow, as if there were nothing inside to hold her up.

I studied her little face. She had a small brown spot on her left cheek.

"Is that a birthmark?" I pointed at the spot.

She touched her cheek. "Yeah. Gip says it's where Jesus kissed me before I left heaven."

"I have one too. I stuck out my lower lip to show her the small white dot I'd had since birth. "See?"

She frowned. "Jesus loves you more."

"Why would you say that?"

"'Cause he kissed you on the lips."

I rubbed my bottom lip and wondered if Jesus really had favorites. If he did, I didn't feel like one of them.

Maggie won six games of Go Fish before she grew bored and plopped onto the sofa. "Will you tell me a story?"

"I don't know any good ones." I yearned to create a story just for Maggie, to make her feel better, safer. But nothing came to me.

Maggie rested her head on a pillow, yellow curls circling her face. She pulled her knees into her chest, her small arms wrapped around Frida, and soon gave in to sleep. Her pale face appeared ghostly in the afternoon's gray light.

I stood at the back window watching the cottonwoods sway to the pulse of the wind. Steel-gray clouds loomed above the village and the scent of rain and earth floated into the house.

When Nana finally got home, her shoulders slumped, making her seem smaller than usual. My heart twisted like *yerba* roots plowing into the ground to see her face so limp and long.

"How is she, Nana?" I whispered as we walked past Maggie.

Nana took me out back and we sat under the long portal. Silence filled the space between us. Even the cicada bugs settled into a hush, saving their song for a sunnier day.

Nana gazed across the yard as though the words she needed hung at the edge of the approaching storm, close enough to taste but too far to touch. "Each of us comes into this life with only a thread of time to live our essence. Some threads are shorter than others.

"Like your father. His thread was short, his journey interrupted. Gip's has been long and it is time for her to leave this world."

Nana patted my leg. "We must help Maggie now, so that her journey is one of joy. We are all she has."

"I don't understand. Can't you heal her?"

"Gip has been sick a long time, *mija*. We knew this day was coming. She has an illness in her brain that cannot be cured, and sometimes she loses her eyesight and falls, like today. And it has only gotten worse." Tears eased down Nana's worn face. "You see, *mija*, when it is your time to leave, nothing can stop that. Even the brightest star in our universe will burn out someday."

"How long does she have?"

"I prayed for another day so that Maggie could say good-bye. I will take her tomorrow. And you too, if you'd like."

We sat hand in hand in the worn leather chairs that, just weeks before, had held the joy and laughter of a birthday celebration. I could almost hear the echoes of that memory on the tips of the breeze, but within minutes rain plunged from the sky and washed them away.

14

BECOMING A BIG SISTER

The next morning, Nana sat silently in the front passenger seat as Mr. Castillo trailed the long line of cars on the highway. Maggie slumped against the window, staring out at the humming traffic.

The city of Albuquerque hurried all around me. There was no whispering wind, no safe cocoon, only black asphalt and concrete buildings. The buildings and bridges had no roots; they just sat on the surface of Earth, temporary tenants of the desert.

I turned my baseball over in my hand, staring at the words. In the afternoon sun, the blue ink appeared even brighter as I traced my finger over the two humps of the letter *M*.

Suddenly M Street seemed a million miles away. And right then, I knew it would never be home.

When we arrived at the hospital, the smell of bad things pushed up my nose. I wondered how long we would have to be here.

Gip lay so still that I thought we were too late. Maggie crawled up into the bed and laid her head on Gip's chest. I had never seen anyone die and I didn't want to. Nana followed me into the hallway.

"It's not right," I said, shaking my head back and forth. "How can this happen—and in a hospital?"

"What do you mean?" Nana asked.

"Gip should die at home, in the village. It's so lonely here, and white. There's no color at all."

Nana wrapped her arms around me, and I wanted so much to let out the hot stinging tears welling up inside of me, but they refused to come.

"You are right, *mija*. We need to take her home."

The smell of death had silently crawled into every crevice of Gip's house. In the distance a dog barked and Frida's ears perked up. Then she blinked her shiny green eyes at me and crawled into my lap. The world grew silent again except for a ticking clock hanging on the wall. I was sitting sprawled on the floor just outside of Gip's bedroom, rolling my baseball beneath my palm. A cool wind floated through an open window and settled beside me.

Frida's belly rose and fell slowly, and in no time she was asleep. Soon my breathing matched hers, and my body became still and quiet. I felt weightless, like I might float away on the lingering wind while Nana and Maggie prayed over Gip. I wanted to thank her for the piece of happiness she had given me when she talked about my dad, but I couldn't bring myself to watch her die.

Gip died on a Saturday. She'd held on through the night, one day longer than Nana had prayed for. Maggie stayed with her until the end, stroking her hair and tickling her face with yarn.

Monday, we bowed our heads to pray as we sat down for lunch.

Nana spoke softly, "Dear Lord, thank you for—"

"I don't like God. He's mean. He takes everyone away." Maggie slithered off her chair and collapsed on the floor sobbing.

I felt so helpless watching her. Nana fell to her knees, scooped Maggie into her arms, and rocked her back and forth as she sang:

"*Sana, sana, colita de rana.*

Si no sanas hoy, sanarás mañana.

Get well and feel better little frog.

If not today then maybe tomorrow."

Nana stroked Maggie's hair, and tears spilled into the yellow swirls as she chanted the same song over and over until Maggie slept.

I helped Nana carry her to my bedroom. "I'm sorry about Gip, Nana."

Nana looped her arm in mine as we walked down the hall. "Death sweeps the earth, but has no power in *el cielo*. Heaven is where we will really know those we love. She is gone only for a short moment. Remember that."

I didn't understand what Nana meant. I felt like my dad had been gone for more than a short moment. Sadness climbed up my bones and I wondered if color would ever come back into this house again.

Two days later, everyone in the village gathered to celebrate Gip's life. She hadn't wanted a burial, so we scattered her ashes in the Rio Grande. Standing on the riverbank as the rushing water pounded at my ears and the scorching sun burned my bare arms, I thought a lot about my dad. I didn't hear any wind whispers that day. Instead, the air felt tight and hot.

After the river ceremony, I passed around trays of *tamales*, *chiles rellenos*, *tacos*, and *pan dulce* to all the friends who came back to Nana's.

"It was a beautiful service, Izzy. Don't you think?" Tía asked as she reached for the last piece of *pan dulce*.

"Yes."

"Reminded me of your papa's funeral. So beautiful to celebrate a good life."

But it didn't seem beautiful at all—just empty.

Later, after all the celebrating, I found Nana on a stepladder, stretching a strip of black crepe paper across the top of the front door.

"What are you doing?" I asked.

"It is an old tradition. Our mourning is over when the sun, wind, or rain takes the paper away."

We stared for a moment at the black strip.

"Did you do this for my dad?"

Nana wrapped her arm around my waist. "*Sí.*"

Nana pointed to the black paper. "I do this because my mama did it, but like the paper, these traditions will some-day float away. There was a time when women went into mourning after a family death and could not be seen in public, only in church."

"I'm glad that tradition floated away. You think it's possible to miss someone you never even knew? Can you ever be really happy after someone dies?"

Nana stepped down and gave me a squeeze. "You will always feel his absence but you can still find joy. Like now, we are sad but that doesn't mean we can't smile or that life won't ever be normal again." She folded the stepladder and set it against the house. "You shouldn't feel bad for moments of joy. Gip would want us to be happy. And so would your papa."

Nana unwound the hose and sprayed water over the garden in the front courtyard; a faint rainbow appeared in the mist. "We must find our way back to joy. Bit by bit. And some of us will find it sooner than others."

I wondered how long it would take Maggie to find her way back. "What will happen to Maggie now?" I asked.

"Gip asked that I raise her. She made legal arrangements a few months ago. We are the only family she has now." Nana looked me in the eye and smiled softly, "You must be a sister to her for the rest of the summer."

I bit my lower lip. A sister? Wasn't a sister someone you were friends with forever and ever, not just a summer? I pinched a small petal from a pink geranium in a nearby pot and caressed its smooth, velvety surface between my thumb and forefinger, careful not to tear it. I wasn't sure if I liked the idea of being a big sister to someone. But even though Gip was gone from this world, the little piece of happiness she had given me on that first day was still in my heart, and I held it as a treasure. I knew I owed it to Gip to be the best sister possible to Maggie.

15

$9.50 Under Budget

Each new day pushed scraps of sadness out of our lives and invited little bits of joy back in. Maggie seemed to absorb the joy the best. Maybe it was Nana's *tortillas,* or maybe she was too young to stay sad for long. Mostly, I think it was the stories Nana whispered to Maggie at night before bed.

One Friday night, Maggie lay in my bed. I learned part of being a good big sister meant sharing my room. Maggie rested her head in Nana's lap and made circles in the air with her yarn for Frida to chase.

"Do you have any new stories about Gip?" she asked Nana.

I sat at my desk and doodled on a story card, unsure of what to write.

Nana stroked Maggie's hair slowly.

"*Sí*. What kind of story would you like to hear?"

"What about one with Gip and Izzy's dad?" Maggie rolled her head to the left and glanced at me before turning back to Nana. "Do you have that kind of story?"

I set my pen down and waited. I never grew tired of Nana's memories.

Nana folded her small hands in her lap. "Well, one summer, Gip wanted to reset the tile floors in her house, but she couldn't do it alone. Gip didn't have much money that year. She received many quotes from different tile layers, and with each new one she would throw her hands in the air and say, 'Can you believe the money these people want? Do they think I'm the queen of England?'

"One night, I went to Gip's with Izzy's mama and papa for a small dinner, and there she was—on her hands and knees with a chisel and hammer—tearing up the whole floor."

I smiled a little at the memory of Mom tearing up our kitchen counter. Maybe Gip had given her the idea.

Nana laughed. "We had all thought we were coming for dinner, but really we spent the whole night tearing up that old floor until we had no choice but to fix the mess we'd made." Nana scooted Maggie's head onto the pillow and tilted her chin upward so she could look her in the eye.

"And that's the kind of spirit Gip had. She always found a way. And that same week she and Izzy's papa went all over Albuquerque searching for leftover tile from building supply stores. She'd said that if he could help her stay under budget, she'd pay him all the money that was left over."

"Didn't she want her floor to match?" I asked.

Nana shook her head. "She didn't want perfection, just comfort."

She continued. "After about a week, Izzy's papa had found tiles on clearance that were a bit damaged, but Gip didn't mind. She said they would just add to the uniqueness of her home."

"Did he get all the tiles under budget?" I asked.

"No. But he never told Gip the actual cost. Instead he asked a few villagers if they would donate some money for her new floor, and when it was all said and done, he had more than enough. Your papa knew Gip was very proud and probably wouldn't take anyone's money, so he kept the villagers' donations quiet. And when he told her he had managed to stay nine-fifty under budget, Gip grabbed her purse and paid him right away." Nana's eyes danced the way they always did when she shared a happy memory. "He spent the next few weeks finding the right fit for each tile and setting them beautifully. Gip always said that wherever you labored with love, a small piece of you would stay there forever. So Izzy, a part of your papa still lives in that house."

My heart swelled with pride as Nana's words wrapped themselves around us like a quilt, each piece sewn together with hope and love.

16

FIREWORKS

By the next Saturday, we'd found a different reason to celebrate. Mateo stood in front of the grill waving the smoke with one arm as he turned the hot dogs.

Nana skulked behind him, watching everything he did like a mama bird. "Do you know what's in those things? A whole lot of factory grown nonsense."

"Come on, Nana. You always cook for us, and now it's the Fourth of July so we're grilling California style." I giggled at how uncomfortable she looked having someone else do the cooking. "We even have fresh watermelon from the farmers' market."

"Is this what your mother feeds you?" she asked.

"Sometimes." I looped my arm in hers as we walked across the lawn toward the shade of the portal. "When we lived on Paradise Place there was this little grill by the laundry room outside that all the tenants shared. But you couldn't use the grill for more than fifteen minutes at a time, so we always cooked hot dogs since they're so fast."

Nana shook her head. "Cooking is an art. It's not about how fast it gets done."

Under the portal, Tía fanned her face with a red, white, and blue striped paper napkin and patted Nana's arm as she sat down next to her. "Oh come on, relax for once." She took two slices of cucumbers from the tray on the table, leaned her head back, and placed them over her eyes. "It's like a day at the beauty shop, right here in your own backyard."

Bubbles floated across the lawn and Frida leapt in the air to catch them. "You have to be faster, Frida," Maggie called from beneath the large cottonwood tree in the middle of the yard where she sat with her bubble wand.

"Look what I have!" Mr. Castillo shouted as he walked across the lawn balancing an armful of colorful boxes, the top one teetering. Mateo and I both ran to meet him and we each took a box.

"Fireworks!" Mateo shouted.

Maggie dropped her bubble wand on the lawn and dashed toward us.

"Cool," I said. "You're allowed to set off your own?"

"Up on the mesa above the village, where there aren't any trees. The whole village comes to watch. It's a tradition," Mateo said.

Mom and I didn't really have any Fourth of July traditions in California—except eating hot dogs. Every year she had a new plan for how to spend the holiday: We'd watch fireworks at the park, the beach, or even a grocery store parking lot because they were offering free hot dogs that year. The summer we lived on Elm Street, we tried to watch them from our third-floor apartment balcony. I had to lean over the edge and really far to the right just to see the tip-tops of the fireworks. That made Mom nervous, so she made me sit and listen to them, instead, while she tried to grill dinner inside on a new skillet she'd just bought.

Now, the familiar smell of hot dogs smoking on the grill made me miss Mom. She would've eaten two, with salsa on top, instead of ketchup or mustard.

After grace, we dug into the dogs, chips and salsa, sliced cucumbers—or what was left of them—and fresh cut watermelon. I watched Nana sprinkle salsa across her dog and smiled.

Tía stood and smoothed her hands over her tight green dress. "This is not at all good for my figure. I look like a sausage! I have to start exercising." As she fanned her face her body jiggled like a column of lime Jell-O. Maggie giggled, and a blob of ketchup dribbled from the side of her mouth.

Mateo glanced toward me and grinned. "Why don't we all have a little game of baseball? That would be good exercise, right, Izzy?"

"But there's only six of us," I said.

"It's enough. I can pitch, you play second and first base." Mateo turned to Maggie. "You can play the outfield with Frida. And the adults will be the other team." He stood and began clearing the table. "We can play at the big clearing by the river since the mesa will be full of villagers waiting for the fireworks show."

Nana snorted. "Are you *loco*? I can barely swing a fly-swatter! And your mama? She might break a nail."

Everyone laughed at this. Except Tía. She tossed her head back with an air of superiority and dabbed at her melting make-up with another napkin. "I'll have you know I played softball in junior high. I even won a trophy."

"Well, you're not going to play in those." Mateo pointed to her high heels. "Do you even own a pair of tennis shoes?"

I stood and looped my arm through Tía's. "Maybe a pair of mine will fit." I led her away from the table, and as I looked over my shoulder at Mateo, I said to Tía, "As a matter of fact, why don't you be on my team? Mateo can be on Mr. Castillo's."

Inside, I collected everything we'd need: a pair of tennis shoes for Tía, Dad's jersey for me, and the baseball for all of us.

Out in the clearing, Nana stood behind a big flat rock we used for home plate. With the bat held in her left hand and resting on her left shoulder, she made the sign of the cross and kissed her fingertips. Mr. Castillo tossed the ball underhand and when Nana swung, the bat flew from her hands and rocketed toward Frida, who dashed under a bush safely.

Nana snickered. "Slipperier than I thought." I retrieved the bat and told Nana to keep a firmer grip. She nudged the dirt with the toe of her tennis shoe and reanchored her stance. "I'm ready."

Mr. Castillo pitched the next three balls high and to the outside.

"Ah, come on, Dad. You're not going to walk her, are you?" Mateo hollered.

"Just warming up my rusty arm." Mr. Castillo wound his arm in looping circles and rubbed his shoulder before he threw another high ball.

"That's the fourth ball." Tía called from the sidelines. "You get to go to first base now!"

Nana picked up her skirt and marched to first base, smiling wide as if she'd hit a home run.

Tía strolled toward home plate like one of those runway models on TV. Maggie followed.

"What're you doing, *mija*?" Mr. Castillo asked.

Maggie crouched low and adjusted her backpack. "I'm going to run for her so she won't get sweaty."

Mr. Castillo shook his head as Tía planted the bat over her shoulder, bent her knees, and sashayed her hips. "Pitch it right to the center."

I don't think Mr. Castillo thought she could hit the ball because he lobbed it right to her. When she pulled the bat back, her raspberry nails glistened in the afternoon sun. She smashed the ball so hard, I worried it might split in two. Up, up, up it flew before crashing down into the outfield.

Maggie bolted toward first base with Frida at her heels. Mateo scooped up the ball and launched it back to Mr. Castillo, who tagged Nana as she scuttled to second.

It was finally my turn. Mr. Castillo wound his arm and pitched the ball underhand.

Strike one.

"Don't go easy on her, Dad!" Mateo called from center field.

I narrowed my eyes at Mateo. Mr. Castillo threw another underhanded pitch and I smacked the ball right over center field.

Tía cheered, "Run, Izzy, run!" as Maggie rounded second, then third, and made it home for our first score. Within seconds, I'd rounded the first base rock and was sprinting toward second. Mateo ran for the ball, which had flown over his head into a bush. My legs burned as I dashed past third and headed for home. Just as I was about to slide into the plate, I saw Mr. Castillo from the corner of my eye catch the ball and run toward the home base rock.

But he was too late. I made it home before he could catch me.

Mr. Castillo gripped his chest then rolled to the ground dramatically, gasping for air. "You definitely hit like your papa," he said between gasps. Then he smiled and handed the baseball to me.

The burn in my legs radiated all over my body and I kissed the baseball. "Thanks."

Nana, Tía, and Maggie hooted and hollered for me.

By the time it was Mateo's turn to bat, I was warmed up and ready to win.

Standing on the little hill of dirt we made for the pitcher's mound, I hiked my leg in the air like the players on TV and pitched the ball to Mateo as hard as I could.

Crack!

A gust of wind reached up, caught the ball, and carried it over my head. I watched it sail beyond the shrubs into a cluster of cottonwoods.

"I'll get it!" I called as I ran toward the trees.

Mateo cheered behind me, "Home run!" And I knew he was right. The ball had zipped too far for me to get it in time to tag Mateo out.

As I plodded through shrubs, a warm wind swept across my back urging me forward.

"Did you lose this?" a voice called out as I scanned the ground.

I glanced up to find a woman standing in front of a small *adobe* house. She had a garden hose in one hand and my baseball in the other.

"Yes," I answered, unsure of whether she was going to throw it or if she expected me to come get it myself.

Stepping closer, I realized I had found the storyteller's home.

"Looks like your ball found its way right to my doorstep," she said as she stared at the words written on the ball. "Magic?"

I wiped a hand across my hot face and swept my tongue over the roof of my dry mouth. "My dad wrote that."

She handed me the ball. "Do you play?"

"Not really. We were just having a game for fun."

She nodded and smiled. "I'm Socorro. I know your nana."

"I'm Izzy."

"Mateo told me you'd be coming by for a story."

"With him and Maggie," I said, gripping the baseball.

"Come tomorrow and make sure to bring your story cards." She turned back to her garden. "You should hurry back. You don't want to miss the fireworks show," she said, glancing toward the dusky sky.

"How did you know?" I stepped back in amazement. "About my story cards?"

With her back to me, she chuckled and said, "I will see you tomorrow."

As I sprinted back, the first of the fireworks exploded across the sky in sparkling streams of white. And for a moment it looked like a hundred magic baseballs were falling from heaven.

17

THE STORYTELLER

Socorro sat in a rocking chair under the sprawling cottonwood in her backyard. Her long skirt reached past her feet, inching to the wet grass.

"Welcome," she said as we entered her back gate and crossed the lawn. Her hair hung in a long braid, a few strands curled across her cheek.

Maggie jumped into Socorro's lap while Mateo and I spread out blankets on the ground in front her. I clutched a small green canvas bag I'd brought from Nana's that held my story cards and knelt on the blanket next to Mateo.

Socorro wrapped her arms around Maggie, like a momma bear around her cub.

"Now, what type of story would you all like to hear today?" she said.

"Maggie wants to hear a ghost story," Mateo said. "A true one."

Before Maggie could protest, Socorro laughed. "Too old to ask for your own ghost stories?"

Mateo leaned back onto his elbows and huffed, "No."

A flock of gray birds swooped across the sky behind her and settled on a branch above. They had come to hear the story too.

"Very well. Today I will tell you a true story." Socorro took several deep breaths and closed her eyes. "Many, many years ago a Mexican family lived near this very village." Her voice rose and fell with the perfect pitch of a bedtime lullaby. She continued to tell us about the family's home that had been destroyed by a fire. "Only one wall and the floor were left, but they didn't have the money to rebuild their home. No one in town would take them in, so the mother, father, and the daughter traveled across the desert looking for help until they came to a small *adobe* where two sisters lived. The sisters gave them shelter and over the course of two weeks the young girl became enchanted with their ways. They made strange brews and spoke magical chants at night. One day the sisters told the family to go home and sleep on the floor of their burned house, where they would find the unexpected. The family thought this was a strange request but had come to trust the sisters and did as they instructed. So they made the journey back. Their first night home they slept on the hard tile floors. The girl woke up in the middle of the night and felt cold hands wrapped around her feet."

Socorro opened her eyes and spoke slowly. "Cold hands are always the sign of the dead come back to visit."

Maggie buried her face in Socorro's neck.

"The next night the girl felt the same cold hands. The family came to find out that the original house had been built by a man who, many believed, got trapped in the wall during the house's construction and died there, standing straight up. When the house burned down, his spirit was finally set free, but he was restless. The girl felt like he had something to show her. So, she went back to the sisters and asked them what to do. They gave her an ancient chant that could only be used once and told her to recite it by the light of the full moon over the river."

Socorro closed her eyes and lifted her face to the sky, as if she were listening to the flutter of an angel in flight.

Finally, she began again.

"Once the spirit was set free, he appeared before the girl and told her to remove six tiles from the floor in her room.

After removing them she found a small wooden box filled with silver. The family celebrated their newfound wealth. Now they could rebuild their home and would never have to worry about money again. The girl was so happy she went back to the sisters in the desert to thank them, but she could not find the house again. It was like it never existed."

Socorro widened her eyes. "But it was not the silver that possessed the true value."

"What was it, Socorro? What?" Maggie bounced impatiently.

Socorro studied the sky. "A storm is coming. We can finish the story tomorrow. You should get home." Maggie stood up and clapped her hands. She hopped from one foot to the other with excitement. "I want to know what happens! Does the girl live happily ever after?"

After folding up our blankets, Mateo nudged me and whispered, "Ask her now."

Socorro stood up and asked if I liked her story.

I slid the canvas bag over my shoulder and nodded. "Especially how she got to talk to the spirit." I couldn't help but think about what it might feel like to talk to my dad. Just once. "Did those things really happen?"

Socorro nodded. "Of course."

Mateo tugged Maggie by the arm. "Come on, we can wait outside."

They shuffled out the side gate as I stood alone under the tree with the storyteller. Socorro stepped closer, glancing at my bag. Her skin was smooth and beautiful. "May I see them? Your story cards?"

After I handed her the cards, she shuffled through them and looked back to me. "You want to know how to tell a story."

My heart jumped faster than a six-legged cricket. "I get started but can't seem to finish. To tie all the pieces together."

"How long do you sit with your stories?"

"Sit?"

"You must be very patient to tell stories. And you must sit with the idea, allowing it to simmer like soup on the stove. You wouldn't go to all the trouble of cutting up the ingredients, throwing them in the pot and expecting it to cook without fire, right?"

"So I'm supposed to cook the story?" I looked at her quizzically.

She unbraided her hair and let it blow in the breeze. "That is a good way to put it. Here's what you should do. When you get an idea for a story, write down the idea. Don't worry about getting anything right. Then think about that idea and let it simmer as you think. Write down ideas, thoughts, anything you can imagine. When I was young I wrote down single words I liked or I'd describe someone I found interesting."

"But—"

"Don't worry about what comes first and what comes last. Just write. The pieces will come together at the right time." She threaded her fingers through her hair and motioned toward the house. "Come inside. I have something to show you."

I tucked my story cards back into the bag and followed her to the screened-in porch, where colored pieces of glass hung suspended by ribbons from the rafters. As she walked by, she ran her hand through them. Their music floated across the porch, jingling like a tambourine.

"What are these?" I asked, reaching to touch them.

"They are truth catchers made of handblown glass. The artist heats the glass in the furnace and uses a pipe to blow and shape the glass into anything she desires. The light reflected by the catchers carries the truth. You see this one?" She pointed to a turquoise square. "This one captures the light of the first full moon of the year."

I peered through a peach-colored heart, but all I saw was Socorro's porch bathed in sunny hues.

"I hear you see things far away, sometimes as far away as the future," I said, my eyes now fixed on the other pieces of sparkling glass.

Her lips curled into a small smile. "And what else do you hear?"

"Mateo says you could see a *tortilla* on the moon."

Socorro chuckled. "And what do you think?"

"I don't really see how a *tortilla* could get to the moon."

Laughing, she pulled down a yellow truth catcher. "Only the right person can see the truth in the light and what it is saying." She handed me the round piece of glass. "I want you to have this."

The golden glass was half the size of a *tortilla*, with several tiny air bubbles suspended inside. But the outside felt smooth, like Nana's hands.

"Hang it near your window. It will catch the light of the sun when it comes into your room. There, you will see the truth." She spoke softly.

"What kind of truth?" I wondered.

"The most important kind of truth. You will know when the time is right."

She crossed the porch and sat in a large easy chair in the corner. "Now, you have another question for me?"

It seemed rude to ask her such a silly question now, after she had been so nice to me—but I really wanted to see Mateo's map. And to prove to him I was brave. "Your hair . . . I want to know . . . how did it get so white?"

Socorro pulled her long hair over her right shoulder and studied it in the fading afternoon light. "I have my father's hair. He was born in the moonlight, as was I." She turned her face to me.

"Every year, during the moon's harvest, the moonbeams turn another strand to white. It is where all my wisdom and power come from."

"Why is that a secret?" I asked.

"It's not. I've just . . . no one has asked before."

I set the truth catcher in the canvas bag. The weight of it anchored the bag to my side as it hung from my shoulder. Before pressing open the screen door, I turned back to Socorro. "Can I come back sometime?"

"Anytime."

When I stepped outside the gate, Mateo lunged forward. "Well? Did you find out the secret of her hair?"

Maggie pulled on the edge of my shirt. "Tell us about her hair, Izzy."

Maggie and Mateo stared at me, waiting, as if my words really mattered. As if nothing in the world was more important.

I leaned forward. "It's the moonlight. She said it gives her wisdom."

"She doesn't see ghosts?" Mateo sounded disappointed.

"No ghosts," I said.

"Is the moonlight going to turn my hair white too?" Maggie asked, her eyes wide with fear.

I knelt in front of her and smiled. "Of course not."

"Why did you take so long?" Mateo asked.

"No reason." But I could feel the reason bumping alongside my hip all the way home.

18

Mateo's Treasure Map

With three weeks left until I had to go back to California, I felt like there were still so many unanswered questions. I hope, hope, hoped the truth catcher would hurry and show me what I needed to see. Maybe it would tell me what the wind had been trying to say for so long, or give me the missing words from my baseball.

I couldn't stop thinking about Socorro's instructions to let my story simmer. So for the next few days, I wrote everything down. How the gold and pink hues reflected off the Sandia mountains, the way the moon looked like a feather floating down from the sky, the way Nana's *tortillas* filled me up, the words I'd heard on the wind.

"What're you doing?" Maggie asked as she skidded into the room with Frida on her heels.

"Just writing." I liked the way that sounded. Like I was official or something.

"What're you writing? Anything about me?" Maggie asked, bouncing on the bed.

"I really don't have a story yet. Just bits and pieces."

"Could you write one for me? I'll be the princess and you can be in it if you want and make sure I get to fly. Oh, and you could talk about the ladder I'm going to build and—"

I raised my hands in the air, laughing. "Hold on. That's a lot of information. When I learn to write a whole story, I promise to write one for you."

"How long is that gonna take?"

I flipped through my stack of cards and shrugged. "As soon as I can make any of these fit together."

Maggie hopped off the bed and leaned over the desk. "So that's all? You just have to fit those cards together?"

"Kind of."

She grabbed a blank card, and with her tongue sticking out one side of her mouth she wrote: *Flyeng Princis.* Then, she handed me the card. "As a reminder case you forget."

I tugged on one of her braids gently. "I won't forget, but Mateo is waiting for our treasure hunt." And to finally show me the map. "You ready?"

I grabbed my canvas bag, which I'd filled with *tortillas*, and darted outside.

Outside, Frida raced ahead, stopping every so often to sniff the ground as if she were hunting for clues. As planned, we met Mateo by the hammock, then followed the dirt-lined path through the trees. My bag bounced against my hip, my ball tucked safely inside.

Mateo walked in front, clutching the map. "Pancho Villa was a famous bandit from Mexico who robbed a U.S. Army wagon and hid the treasure somewhere near here."

"Mateo, how do you know about the treasure?" Maggie asked, walking behind us.

"Well, my father told me, and his father told him."

"Why do you think no one has found it?" I asked.

Mateo put his arm around my shoulders. He leaned into my ear and whispered, "Because ghosts guard the treasure."

I allowed him to linger for a moment before I pulled away.

"The legend says that Pancho Villa killed his guards and threw them in with the treasure so that it would be guarded forever," he continued.

"Are they gonna get me, Izzy?" Maggie ran to me and put her arm around my waist.

I gave Mateo a dirty look. "No. Don't be silly. Ghosts can't hurt you, Maggie."

Mateo patted the top of Maggie's head, "No one will get you. I'm the one who's going to go after it." He gave me a crooked smile. "I heard someone found where the treasure's buried, but was too afraid of the ghosts to uncover it. He was the one who made the map. My great grandfather won it from him in a poker match."

Putting out my hand expectantly I said, "So a deal's a deal. I proved I'm brave, so, show me the map."

Mateo hesitated, but then, head bent low, handed me the map. "For you, brave Izzy."

I stood straight and winked at Maggie as I took it. It was a wrinkled, brown paper, torn at the edges. It looked more like a small wadded-up lunch sack than a treasure map. Mateo stood over my shoulder as I scanned the words and child-like drawings. In the upper-right corner was a compass rose pointing in the four directions. At the center of the map were five squiggle lines, a hand drawing of three trees to the east of the squiggles, mountains above the trees, and a big *X* next to a cluster of bushes. At the bottom of the map were these barely legible words scribbled in cursive:

There you must soar with fire, to see the treasure you desire.

I held the map up to the sun that was peeking out from behind silvery clouds.

"Does it make any sense to you?" Mateo asked. "I know it's to the east of the river. But what do you think those words mean?"

"I'm not sure," I said.

Mateo kicked at the dirt. "There must be something I'm missing."

"Well the *X* is near a bunch of bushes, we know that, right?" I said.

Mateo huffed and leaned in closer. He smelled of soap and water.

"I want to help." Maggie reached for the map but Mateo pulled it from me before she could touch it.

Maggie's bottom lip quivered and I shot Mateo a look that said, *give it back, or else.* "No one ever said she couldn't see it, just not touch it, right?" I asked.

Mateo reluctantly handed it over. Maggie smiled and stepped closer, gazing at the treasure map. "Hey, they can't write very good."

"Who can't?" Mateo asked.

"Whoever drew this. That's a backwards *B*." She pointed to the small cluster of bushes. "It's supposed to be one line up and two loops to the right." She sang the words. "That's what my teacher teached me."

Mateo swept Maggie into his arms and kissed the top of her head. "You're a genius. That's it. Now we just have to find a bunch of bushes shaped like a *B*."

I scanned the thicket of trees and bushes. "You know how many bushes there are around here?" I said.

Frida licked her paws, seemingly bored with all our talk of treasure maps and letters.

"I'm hungry." Maggie said as she took a pile of treats from her pocket. Frida stood on her hind legs and waited for Maggie's commands to sit, roll over, and shake. With each successful trick she gulped down a peanut butter treat.

"Come on. Where's your adventurous spirit?" Mateo raised his eyebrows at Maggie.

Maggie rubbed her stomach. "Mine's eating my tummy."

I handed her and Mateo each a *tortilla* from my bag. He held it up to the sky for inspection. "Who made this? It sure doesn't look like one of Nana's *tortillas*."

"Well, then don't eat it if you don't like the way it looks." I threw my head back and walked in front of him. "Can *you* make *tortillas*?"

He laughed and jogged to catch up to me. "Is everyone from California as funny as you?"

"Only about their treasure."

Bowing, he said, "And the brave Izzy can make a joke."

Suddenly, the wind swirled through the trees, whispering in my ear. *Come.*

"I have an idea. I'll walk south along the river, and try to find a cluster of bushes shaped like a *B*, and you can walk north. We'll cover more ground that way," I said quickly.

Maggie grabbed my hand. "Will you be sad, Izzy, if I go with Mateo? I just think he can fight off ghosts better."

"It's fine." I breathed a sigh of relief, grateful to be alone to follow the wind.

The wind had a raspy, impatient tone. Thirsty trees bent over the edge of the upper riverbank kissing the heads of white wildflowers sprouting near the sand. I imagined my mother as a little girl saving the fish and giggled to myself. Following the river downstream, I threw rocks and twigs along the way. The stretched-out clouds overhead cast long shadows across the water.

In the distance, something white caught my eye. I stomped along a shaded path overgrown with woody branches until I reached a small wooden cross. It was surrounded by piles of red-and-white plastic roses. The wind twisted through a thicket of trees, finally settling into a faint breeze that stroked my cheek.

Bella.

"Why did you call me here? And why do you keep calling me 'Bella'?"

I knelt down and swept my fingertips across the top of the crooked cross. Was someone buried here? Why was there no name across the front? The breeze lingered, waiting to see what I might find.

My heart beat to the rhythm of the pulsing river: quiet and steady. The gentle murmurs of the swaying trees, the gurgling river, and the faint breeze created a symphony of sounds that sang out, *you belong here.*

I laid on my stomach and noticed something silver peeking from beneath the roses. Sweeping the flowers aside, I found a small metal box. The latch was locked.

Maggie and Mateo's voices came to me on the wind, and soon they were upon me.

"Did you find anything?" Mateo asked. Small scraps of hope fell from his words.

I held up the box. "This was here." I sat back on my knees in front of the cross.

"What's inside?" Mateo said.

I shrugged. "It's locked." I looked back to the cross. "Is this a grave?"

"It's a *descanso*," Maggie said. "It's for dead people."

I scooted away quickly.

"Well, not exactly. It marks the place of someone's death," Mateo said.

"Whose is it?" I asked.

But in my heart I already knew the answer.

19

BELLA AND THE
MARSHMALLOW GHOST

When Maggie and I got home, the house smelled of fresh green chile *enchiladas* and chicken soup. I was happy to find Nana in the kitchen rolling out *tortillas*. Maybe things were finally getting back to the rhythm I had gotten used to—and liked.

Maggie fell asleep in Nana's room with Frida, so I hurried into the kitchen to talk to her alone.

"Can I help you, Nana?"

"Of course, *mija*." Nana set a bowl of dough in front of me. I began to roll small balls and set each aside.

Turn. Press. Roll. Turn. Press. Roll.

One *tortilla* looked like it might turn out the way I wanted it to. But the harder I tried, the more it stuck to the counter, and before I knew it, it looked like the letter *D*.

For death. *Descanso.* Dwell. I pushed the dough into a ball and rolled it across the counter. With a sigh I watched Nana press and roll with perfect rhythm.

"I found something at the river today," I said. "The wind called me there."

Nana turned back around to finish the dishes in the sink. "What did the wind say?" she asked as if it was the most normal thing in the world to talk to the wind.

I took a deep breath and thought about my words carefully. "It led me to a white cross. Maggie called it a *descanso.*"

"Come. Let us sit." Nana led me to the living room and lit the candle in her Santa Maria altar. Silver medals and cards with Mary's picture filled the space. In the back was a wood carved statue of Mary, like the ones I saw in church, with two plastic red roses laid at her feet.

"A *descanso* is the marker of an interrupted journey. When life is cut short. I put it there," Nana said.

"My father's," I whispered.

Nana nodded.

A million whispers glided down my spine.

Nana continued. "It is only a marker. It is part of our tradition to honor and celebrate the life of someone we love. I placed the marker there to honor him."

"Is that where he . . . drowned?" I asked as I watched the flickering candle wick burn so low I thought it might burn out.

Nana rested her small hand on my leg. "*Sí, mija.*"

I reached for my bag at the foot of the sofa and pulled the box out. "So this was his too?"

Nana scanned the metal box and smiled. "I left it there for you. Your papa would want you to have it."

"But why didn't you just give it to me?"

"I knew you would find it when the time was right. It wasn't up to me to decide."

I cradled the box as if it were a newborn baby. It felt light and hopeful. "It's locked."

"*Un momento.*" Nana disappeared down the hallway, reappearing a few minutes later. She handed me a small silver key.

As I stared at the key in the palm of my hand, I whispered, "Thank you."

Needing to be alone, I carried the box to Estrella and set it on the bed.

I carefully inserted the key into the lock and unlocked the box. When the lid lifted, my eyes at last glimpsed the face I had searched for. A face like my own.

Lifting the photo from the box, I studied his deep-set green eyes. My eyes. He squinted into the sun, his smile wide and welcoming. He stood on a baseball field with a bat swung over his left shoulder and a baseball in his right hand. My baseball!

My breath quickened as I studied the picture closely. No matter how hard I tried I couldn't read the words written across the front of the ball in the photo. But one thing was certain, there were two words floating between *because* and *magic*.

Beneath the photo was a small ivory note card. I opened the note; it was dated the week before I was born.

How is our little girl doing? I can hardly wait to meet Bella.

Did the wind have the right girl after all? I folded a corner of the card back and forth trying to make sense of it all before turning back to the note.

Will be home soon.

I love and miss you both.

Jack.

My head felt like it might float out the window, just like a marshmallow ghost.

20

THE SHATTERED TRUTH

Nana left a note on the kitchen table the next morning, telling me she was shopping in the village. She drew a smiley face and an arrow pointing to a plate of bacon-and-egg *burritos*.

I grabbed one from the plate and strolled back to Estrella. When the phone rang, I expected Mateo or Nana's voice.

"Izzy?"

"Mom?"

She laughed on the other end. "I'm so happy I got you. The connection is awful here."

I didn't know whether to be happy or mad. "I need to talk to you . . ."

"I can't wait to see you. Just a couple more weeks. Do you hear the rain?"

Her voice reminded me how much I missed her.

"Why couldn't you tell me? About my name? About Dad?"

Static.

"Hello? Mom? Are you there?" I tapped and shook the phone. "Mom?"

Silence.

There was so much I wanted to ask, but reaching her seemed more impossible than sending a *tortilla* to the moon.

"Izzy, help, help! I'm bleeding!" Maggie hollered.

I hung up the phone and ran out to the living room, banging my head on the bedroom doorframe on my way out.

"Let me see. Where?"

Maggie leaned on the sofa crying. She opened her mouth wide. Blood oozed from her gums.

I laughed. "It's just a tooth. Is it loose?"

She shook her head and cried some more. "No. I can taste it. I'm dying!"

I walked her to the bathroom sink and let her spit a few times. "You aren't dying. I promise. Do you want me to pull it out?"

Her eyes widened. "My tooth? No, I want to keep it!"

"But Maggie, it has to come out otherwise the new one can't come in. And don't you want the tooth fairy to visit you tonight?"

"Fairy?"

I nodded and she let me pull her front tooth.

"Hey, it didn't hurt," she said with her new toothless smile. After she swished warm water around her mouth a few times she pushed her tongue through the hole and giggled. "It feels funny, slippery." Then she turned to Frida. "Do I look any different?"

Looking at Maggie with her missing tooth reminded me of that first day in our new apartment on M Street, the day I found the photo of myself as a six-year-old on the beach with Mom. The same day I found the baseball. Now it seemed so, so long ago.

Frida stood on her hind legs as Maggie smiled down at her, and for a moment I thought she might bark.

Maggie and I sat on the edge of my bed, planning a celebration for her lost tooth.

"Can we have ice cream, Izzy?"

"Of course. We'll have a tea party with ice cream and *sopaipillas.*"

Maggie squealed and hugged me. "Can we bring your glass sun? It would look so pretty hanging from the tree."

"Uh-uh. Socorro told me to leave it in the window."

Maggie reached up and took it from the east window where it had hung since the day at Socorro's.

"It's so pretty though."

"I said no!"

She glared back at me defiantly. "It's just a piece of glass." She stood up on the bed and held the truth catcher up to her face, giggling. "Everything is yellowy."

"Put it down." I reached over to grab it from her. But she pulled back, and the truth catcher tumbled from her hands in slow motion like a giant snowflake twirling from the sky.

It crashed to the *Saltillo* floor before I could catch it.

I stared at the shattered pieces. The broken tiles all over the kitchen floor back on M Street flashed through my mind. "You broke it!"

Maggie jumped off the bed and dropped to the ground, "Oh, I'm sorry, Izzy. I didn't mean to." She tried to pick up all the pieces. "Socorro might give you another one."

"No she won't. It's one of a kind." Anger swelled inside. "Just leave me alone!"

"But our celebration—"

"Just forget it. There's nothing to celebrate."

I gaped at all the broken pieces. Now I would never see what Socorro promised.

Hours later, twisted feelings bounced inside me, unsure where to land. I thought about all that Maggie had lost, and felt mad at myself for being so mean to her. Then the thought of my shattered truth catcher reminded me of all the pieces of stories Mom hadn't told me about my father, and now my name, and I got angry all over again. But with each hour that passed, it was harder to apologize, so I just stayed mad and Maggie stayed in my room the rest of the afternoon.

When Nana got home I was chomping down my third *tortilla* in the kitchen, hoping each one would make me feel better. I didn't even bother to slather butter on this last one. Cold and plain did just fine.

Nana set down an armload of brown paper grocery sacks. "*Hola*, Izzy. You all right?"

Shaking my head, I picked at the brown spots on the *tortilla* and my stomach began to ache.

"What is it? What's wrong?"

"Maggie broke my truth catcher! The one Socorro gave me." I blinked hard trying to keep my tears from falling.

"Now I'll never see the truth." I buried my face into my folded arms on the table.

Nana sat next to me and stroked my hair. "What truth would you like to see?"

I didn't answer for a long time. Then I raised my head and wiped under my eyes with my fingertips. "I don't know. I'm just tired of it coming in pieces." I leaned my elbow on the table and rested my head against my hand. "Like my name. Why didn't you tell me?"

Nana smiled softly. "But I did. I gave you the key to the box." She folded my half-eaten *tortilla* in half and pressed along the seam, but it didn't split like the store-bought ones.

"But what does it mean? Is my real name Bella?

"This is a lot for you to think about. That is why it comes in pieces. You can better absorb it then." Nana reached for my hand. "Your father and mother named you Bella before you were born," she said softly.

"Then, because of all that happened, your mother chose Isadora instead, which is also a beautiful name."

Was this last part supposed to make me feel better? I flicked a speck of *tortilla* from the table.

"The name you are given is not as important as what you carry inside here." She pressed her palm over her heart.

"And that's the truth. If you are meant to see another truth, you will."

"But how? Socorro gave me the truth catcher to show me the most important truth. And now that it's broken I'll never know."

Nana stood and leaned against the kitchen counter. "My nana once told me that anything that is broken can be mended."

I shook my head. "The pieces are too small and sharp to put back together. I wouldn't even know which piece went where."

"You know, *mija*, sometimes we need to see things from a different point of view. You are still looking at the truth catcher as a whole. But you see, it has only changed shapes." She pointed toward the floor. "Look at the *Saltillo* tile. What do you see?"

I looked down. "Bumpy tile."

Nana chuckled. "Ah, Izzy. Look closer. Each tile is unique. You see, the grooves and markings are different on each one. And together, when set at the right angle and lined up just right, they make one floor."

Nana stood up and ran her small fingers over the top of my head. "Try not to see the truth catcher as you think it should be. Instead study two pieces at a time to see if, or how, they connect. That's how you will remake it."

"I'll never be able to fix it and I'll never see the most important truth now!"

I ran through the garden, down the hill to nowhere. I just wanted to run. Fast and far. When I reached the hammock, I stopped and fell back into its comfort. Tears stung my eyes and the air felt still and sad. Frida jumped onto my lap, uninvited.

"Did Maggie send you to beg? Forget it. Go back and tell her I'm still mad."

Frida turned in circles, then finally settled down with her head on her paws. Beneath that long dark brow, her green eyes softened.

"You want to stay, huh?" Rubbing between her ears, I said, "You're lucky you're just a cat." I covered my mouth quickly. "Sorry, I meant dog. It's just a word. It doesn't mean anything." I stroked her ears and listened to her purr. "I guess we're the same that way. My real name is Bella. My dad named me." I turned my face to the side and lifted my chin. "What do you think? Do I look like a Bella or an Izzy? Definitely not Isadora."

Frida rolled onto her back and rolled her long tongue out the side of her mouth panting. In that light she looked more like a dog than I'd ever thought before.

"Isadora. Isa. Bella . . . Maybe I can be Izzy and Bella, Frida," I whispered. "Isabella Reed Roybal."

Frida walked across my chest and licked my cheek. "Yeah, I like the ring of it too."

I imagined what my dad's voice might sound like, and how he would call after me. "Bella!" he'd say. "You want to play a game of catch?"

Sunlight spilled through the trees, and as I swung the hammock, my shadow shifted across the earth. I thought about Dad resetting the tiles on Gip's floor, how he was able to make the pieces fit together.

A small dove landed on a branch above me. She rested for only a moment before she flew away, joining a flock of birds that looked like little pieces of black paper floating on the wind. They reminded me of the pieces of my story that were still missing. I wanted to be a bird, to fly away to wherever I chose. To touch the clouds and the sky, to be closer to the wind.

I gazed at the words written across the ball. "If only you were here, Dad," I whispered. "You could tell me the missing words and how to put the truth catcher back together."

I thought about the girl from Socorro's story and how she brought the spirit back with a chant. The idea simmered at first, then came to a boil the more I thought it might be possible.

It might be my only chance.

I looked up at Frida. "What do you think? Could it work? Maybe I need a sign to know for sure."

Frida perked her ears.

"Here's the deal: I'm going to throw the ball as high as I can, and if I catch it then I'm going to get the chant from Socorro."

Straddling the hammock, I threw the ball toward the sky. Hope rose in my chest as it fell. But then the ball stopped, landing in the tree directly above, wedged in the branches.

I let out the breath I'd been holding. Just as I collapsed back into the hammock, a warm breeze stroked my bare arms, sending goose bumps from the back of my neck all the way down to my toes. And then, in one sudden gust, the breeze flew into the tree and shook the branches mightily.

The baseball fell into my lap.

21

CALLING DAD

I told Mateo about my plan to call Dad's spirit. That I'd gotten a sign. At first he didn't want to help me until I reminded him of the promise he had made me the day at the ghost trail.

"How is that ever gonna work?" he asked.

"Because it happened in the story Socorro told us and she said the story was true, so that makes it possible. Right?"

Mateo shrugged. "Yeah, I guess."

"Look, I'll talk to Socorro and ask her all the details. Tonight is supposed to be a full moon so you just meet me at the hammock at midnight and we will go to the river."

Mateo didn't say a word.

"Are you going to help me or not?" I insisted.

"Yeah, I'll be there. I just hope you know what you're doing."

I visited Socorro that day and asked her if the chant was real.

"Why do you need to know?" she asked.

"I need to talk to my dad. I can't wait for the right time anymore. I'm tired of waiting. And if the story is true, if the girl from the story can bring back a spirit, I can too, right?"

She smiled softly and asked about the truth catcher. When I told her it broke she pinched her eyebrows together.

"I'm really sorry. It was an accident," I said.

"Yes. I know." She paused for a moment. "Follow me. I will give you the chant."

She handed me a folded piece of paper. "Would you like to hear the rest of the story now?"

"Maybe another time. I really have to go."

I grabbed the paper and stepped toward the door. "Do you think he'll know who I am?"

"He has always known you."

Before she could say another word I flew out the door and ran home as fast as I could. My legs felt strong as I glided across the earth, up and down the hills, and through the trees. My long hair blew free in the wind and the sun kissed my smiling face.

That night after Maggie and Nana had gone to sleep, the house settled into a peaceful lull. I had told Maggie I didn't want to sleep with her anymore and made a bed for myself on the sofa to make sneaking out easier. If she wanted Estrella so badly, then she could have it. I had more important things to think about.

The brilliant light of the full moon sat high above the canopy of trees. Close to midnight, I looked out the window, listening as the wind rustled through the leaves, inviting me outside.

Come, Bella.

I traced my fingers over the word *magic* on my baseball. "I'm going to need it tonight," I whispered, tucking the ball into the large center pocket of my sweatshirt.

All the *santos* on the walls stared at me as I made my way through the house, and guilt sank in my gut like a raw piece of *tortilla* dough. Once I reached the back door, I eased it open and closed it carefully behind me. As I dashed toward the hammock, the wind began to howl, trees bowed, and lightning split the sky. My bravery melted away with each step.

What if something went wrong? I shook this thought from my mind. I had waited so long for answers that kept coming in pieces. By the time I reached Mateo I was out of breath.

"Are you all right?" he asked.

I nodded. "Yeah. Come on let's go."

"Izzy, maybe we should wait until after this storm."

"I'm not waiting anymore. If you want to go back you can."

Mateo shook his head. "No. I made a promise."

We scuttled through the brush and over the rocks until we reached the winding river. But when we got to the *descanso* I remembered something from Socorro's story.

"Socorro's story said the chant has to be said over the water, remember?"

Mateo turned upstream. "The bridge."

We ran toward the bridge as the wind continued to screech across the valley and thunder boomed across the sky. We didn't have much time.

"The water is so high—are you sure it's safe?" Mateo asked.

I nodded and turned toward the bridge. He caught me by the elbow. "Do you want me to go with you?"

"No. I need to do this part alone."

He released my arm. "I'll wait for you on the riverbank."

The bridge hung only a foot or so above the water and swung back and forth as I walked toward the middle, balancing myself on the handrail of slick rope. The rushing waters splashed my feet, but I continued to the center of the bridge.

The full moon gave just enough light to see the water glimmering below as it rushed toward the ocean. When the bridge swung back and forth in the wind I didn't feel so brave anymore, but I had come too far to turn back.

I had already memorized the chant on the paper. I turned to the west, took a deep breath, and said, "Spirit of the west! Source of the sunset and death, the place of sorrow, and empty deserts. I call back what I have been called to let go."

I turned to the east. "Spirit of the east! Source of the sunrise, and the place of beginnings. I call back—"

"Izzy?"

I turned toward Mateo standing on the riverbank only a few yards away.

"What!"

"Did you hear something? I think someone's here."

My insides began to tremble as rain plunged from the sky. "But I haven't finished yet. He can't be here already."

Suddenly, Frida ran onto the bridge with Maggie right behind her.

"Maggie! What are you doing here?"

"I wanna talk to Gip and my mom. I heard you tell Mateo what you were gonna do and I wanna do it too."

The anger that had settled deep into my gut exploded. "I can't believe you followed us here. You ruin everything. Now go home!"

Mateo stood at the entrance of the bridge. "What's gotten into you, Izzy? She can't walk back alone in the dark. And it's pouring. We have to go back."

I pushed the rain from my eyes. "Why not? She managed to come here alone."

"Come on, Maggie. I'll walk you back," Mateo shouted over the rain as he stepped onto the wet planks of wood.

"I don't wanna go home. I wanna see Gip!"

Frida zigzagged around my legs, her gray fur standing up in dark, spiky peaks. My anger must have run all the way down to my feet because I jerked my leg forward and nearly kicked her into the river. Frida leapt back and flipped over the side of the bridge.

"Frida!" Maggie shouted.

Frida dangled off the bridge like a flailing fish on a hook, half her body clinging to the bridge, the other half dangling into the water. She clawed and scratched to save herself. When I lunged forward to pull her to safety, the bridge bent and swung dangerously as the wind howled across the night sky.

"Izzy, be careful!" Mateo shouted.

I tried to grab hold of the rope and balance myself. "Maggie, stand still. Don't let go of the rope!"

I stretched toward Maggie with one hand, while securing myself with the other. Panic flashed in her eyes and I knew she wasn't listening to me. She let go of the rope and leaned down to save Frida. With a splash she fell into the water.

Her small voice cried out, "Izzy!"

Before I knew it, Maggie's light yellow hair was swallowed by the dark currents of the Rio Grande and Frida was nowhere to be seen.

Without another thought, I jumped into the river. "Maggie!" The rush of the cold water pushed its way into my bones. From the corner of my eye I saw Mateo leap into the river too.

I tried to keep my head above the water, but the river danced to a strong, powerful beat and I bounced along like a skipping pebble, bumping my tailbone and legs against rocks and sharp branches. The rain was coming down fast and hard now and I couldn't see where I was headed.

Darkness hugged the valley and joined in the river's dangerous dance. "Mag—"

The water rushed into my mouth, sucking out the sweet summer air. Suddenly the river grew deeper and I plunged farther into the blackness.

I reached out for anything I could grab hold of. Memories of swimming in the ocean flashed across my mind. I remembered how the force of the crashing waves sent me tumbling. "Remain calm and let the force of the wave grow tired," Mom always told me.

All of a sudden I felt a hand that must have been Maggie's grab onto me and pull me farther under the water. I struggled to reach the air. The sky seemed so dark now and the harder I tried to reach for it, the deeper into the water I sank.

Dear God. Please help me. I thought about Mom and Dad. I didn't want to die. Somehow I rose above the waterline, but as soon as I caught a breath, Maggie's desperate little body climbed on top of me and shoved me back under. As my head felt fuzzy and my body grew faint, I began to imagine Nana's kitchen.

I smelled the sweet, spicy scents floating from the oven; I heard the musical echoes of her laughter, and I saw streams of light dancing across her kitchen walls. The light grew brighter and Maggie's grabbing arms were pulled away as I drifted closer to the glow all around me.

Just as I was about to let go of the fight, I felt cold hands surround my waist and push me up to the surface.

Mateo. He'd found me.

With each gulp of air, the radiance of the light faded. I felt the slow lapping of water and the sweet, easy motion of my body floating with the current. I lay still and let the force carry me safely to the water's edge.

Then everything went black.

22

The Missing Words

I opened my eyes slowly and lay still. My body wouldn't move. Images rippled across my mind; Nana's orange and lavender scented hands combed through my hair, Mom floated beneath a waterfall. She called for me, but I couldn't answer. Maggie looped her soft pinky around mine. Was I dead? Had the wind carried me to heaven?

"Batter up!" a man's voice called out.

The world as I knew it had fallen away. I blinked twice and suddenly found myself standing next to home plate with a bat in my hand. Men in baseball uniforms spread out across the field and on each base. A crowd cheered in the stands behind me.

The first ball rifled past my waist. I winced. "Striiiike!" the umpire's voice called out.

A small thrill ran up my spine. I knew I could hit the next one. Gripping the bat, I inched closer to home plate.

A voice behind me whispered, "Hey, if you're gonna hit the ball, you have to step up and take the swing. Don't hold on so tight. Let the bat ease into your hands."

I looked over my shoulder at the catcher. Wasn't he on the other team? Shaking my head, I propped the bat over my right shoulder and bent my knees.

"Relax. Step up and take the swing," he said.

The next ball whirred by. I didn't even see it coming.

The catcher stood and leaned forward. "The ball comes at different speeds—never the same pitch twice. You can't really be prepared for what you're going to get." He squatted and punched his mitt. "The key is to keep your eyes on the ball the whole time."

I nodded.

"And then hit it with everything you've got." He pointed to the twinkling lights. "Aim for the stars."

Something inside urged me forward. I stepped beside home plate and focused intently on the pitcher. Above him, the first stars appeared against the last light of day like little white shadows. I squinted one eye and pointed the bat to the brightest star I could find.

Thunderous cheers rose from the crowd.

I settled into a batter stance, my eyes narrowed, my heart determined. The ball came slow this time, but curved at the last second. Time slowed and the ball rotated and twisted before me. Wait. Wait. Wait. *Smash!*

Shocked, I stood unmoving as I watched the ball fly toward the star.

"Run!" The catcher pushed me toward first base.

I threw the bat to the ground and sprinted. As I rounded first base and dashed past second, cheers erupted from the crowd. My feet slammed the ground, creating clouds of dirt. My lungs hurt. As I turned third, I could see the ball falling down from the heavens.

I pushed my legs, forcing them to move even though they screamed to stop. Home plate was only a few feet away. I threw my body down and slid toward the base. Just as my fingers swept the edges, the ball crashed into the dirt field. A great light blinded me. The crowd and players evaporated, like water on hot cement.

Dust choked my throat and masked my eyes. I rose to my feet and blinked twice. The moon hung high in the sky and silence embraced the field.

"Good game," a voice said.

I spun around. The catcher stood before me. He slowly peeled back the mask. I saw his smile first, and then his eyes. The same as mine.

A hundred church bells sounded in my ears. "Dad?"

He nodded. "I've been waiting for you." He reached for my hand and smiled. Soft lines formed around his eyes. "You sure can smack a ball."

As I blinked, dizzy and confused, he walked me toward a bench in the middle of the ball field and we sat beneath the stars. I settled against the smooth wooden bench and clasped my hands together, trying to make sense of what had to be a dream. I forced the words from my mouth. "Have I gone to heaven?"

He threaded his hair with his fingers. "It's a little closer to Earth than heaven. It's a visiting place."

"This baseball field?"

"It's different for everyone."

I felt the weight of his stare.

"Do you . . . like it here?"

Folding his arms across his chest he leaned back. "I'd rather be with you."

Running my hand along the edge of the bench a splinter got caught in my skin. "Me too."

I poked at the splinter. "Why did Mom keep you from me?"

He touched my shoulder lightly. "She was only trying to protect you."

"From what?" I said turning my face to him. "From you?"

"She didn't want you to feel her kind of pain. She wanted things to be easier for you."

"But nothing has been easy. Why couldn't she just tell me?"

He stroked my hair lightly. "Maybe sending you to New Mexico was her way of sharing the truth. Maybe it was a story she just couldn't tell herself. But a story for you to discover."

Could he be right? Had Mom sent me to the village to learn the truth? Was this her way of finally sharing the answers to all my questions? Is that why she told Nana to go slowly and wondered if I'd forgive her? In that moment it was like all the broken pieces had been glued together. The summer night air warmed me and I knew he was right. I was tired of carrying all that anger and confusion.

I reached into my sweatshirt pocket and handed him the baseball. "I'm glad you left this behind."

He smiled staring at the words. "I hit the most important home run of my life with this ball."

"What happened?"

"Your mom married me because of this." He tossed me the ball. "Ask her to tell you the story."

"But she won't."

"I think things will be different now." He winked at me and grinned. "Tell her you know the missing words."

"I do?"

He leaned over and whispered. "Because love is magic."

"Love." I repeated the word softly. It seemed so simple now. I thought about what Nana had said about magic and how it meant special and enchanting. How sometimes you can't see it but you can feel it.

"Batter up!" A voice boomed from a loudspeaker.

Dad turned toward home plate. "I have to go now." Gently, he swept my hair from my face.

My throat swelled. "Don't go. Please."

Rising from the bench, he held his hand out to me.

I folded my hand in his and pulled myself up into his arms.

He released me and looked into my eyes. "I love you."

As I watched him walk toward home plate, I knew I would see him again. Someday. He turned and winked at me. For a split second I saw a stadium and a cheering crowd. Then a gentle wind swept across my face.

I sank onto the field and stared at the thousands of stars now cast across the sky. My eyes burned. I only wanted to close them for a moment. One short moment would make it better. Instead, I slept. A deep peaceful sleep, where I floated between this world and the next in perfect silence.

AN ARMFUL OF DREAD

"Izzy. Izzy?"

I stirred. Don't call me back. Let me stay here.

"Izzy!"

Opening my eyes to the chilly, dark bank of the river, I blinked back the darkness. The wind had disappeared and I rolled onto my side and sat up.

Mateo was at my side; he helped me to my feet. "You scared me half to death." He squeezed me.

I let him hold me as I rested my groggy head on his shoulder. The events of the night began to unfold slowly. "You jumped in to save me."

"I tried, but the river carried you farther and farther away."

"You risked your life."

Mateo pulled away from me. "I've been swimming here my whole life. Me and the river have grown up together. I was scared you were hurt but your nana said that these waters would never take you—"

Suddenly, I was jolted from my dreamlike state. "Nana. Maggie! Where's Maggie? Is she hurt?"

"She's with Nana. But Izzy . . ." Before Mateo could utter another word, I ran up the riverbank toward the flashing red lights in the distance.

The screeching sound of sirens filled the valley and reminded me of the distant, outside world. I found the paramedics setting Maggie on the stretcher and carrying her away. Nana followed behind them until she saw me. When I closed the distance between us and we stood face to face, I saw something in her eyes that scared me: emptiness.

"Nana, I'm so sorry."

I collapsed into her and she wrapped her arms around me. Hot stinging tears streamed down my face. One tear after the other fell. Nana pulled back and wiped her hand across my cheek.

The pale moonlight shone across Nana's face, making her look like a ghost.

"How's Maggie?" I said as my feet sank into the muddied earth.

"The paramedics have stabilized her. *Gracias a Dios.* Are you in any pain?" Nana said.

"I'm not hurt," I said. "But why did you say the waters wouldn't take me?"

Nana gazed toward the full moon. "Socorro told me about a vision she had. You were fighting the pull of the waters, but you would find your way back to the village, unharmed."

"Did she say anything about Maggie?"

Nana shook her head.

"Can't you heal Maggie?"

Nana took a deep breath. "I eased the water from inside her and did what I could."

"This is all my fault! I should never have tried to . . . I feel so stupid."

"Izzy, I must go to the hospital."

"But Nana. I don't want to stay alone. Besides I have so much to tell you. I—"

"No, Izzy. I have no time to talk about this now. You cannot come with me. Now go home; I will call you soon." She turned to Mateo. "Please take care of her."

Mateo nodded.

I watched Nana push her way up the riverbank toward the ambulance. She turned and gazed at me. Her eyes had the same sad faraway look as Mom's the day she put me on the plane and waved good-bye.

"Your mama called late tonight. She knows something is wrong." And then she was gone.

I searched the night sky. Was he up there? Could he see me? The night's events played out in slow motion and I trembled from the inside out.

"All this is my fault. I was too impatient and now Maggie is hurt because of me," I told Mateo. Hot stinging tears ran down my cheeks. The wind dried them as fast as I cried them.

"Where's Frida?"

"I found her right after I got Maggie out of the water. Never knew a cat could swim like that."

"You mean *dog*. Where is she now?"

Mateo motioned to the right, where Frida was curled up under the moonlight, her small head resting on her paws as she waited to see what we would do next. I walked over and lifted her into my arms. "I'm sorry, girl."

She rolled her head across my hand as I scratched between her ears. I kept my eyes fixed on Frida and said to Mateo, "You saved Maggie?"

"As soon as I jumped in I lost sight of you, but then I saw Maggie surface. When I finally caught her, she had swallowed a lot of water." He shook his head. "It was that back sack of hers that saved her. It got caught on a rock and slowed her down long enough for me to get there." He put his hands into his pockets and rocked back and forth on his heels and toes. "I yelled as loud as I could, and in a flash your nana was here helping Maggie breathe."

"Then what happened?"

"She sent me to search for you. I was so relieved when I saw you crawl to the water's edge."

"I didn't crawl out of the water though."

"Yeah you did. I saw you."

"It was my dad. He pushed me out of the water. He was there, Mateo. He talked to me and everything. We played baseball . . ."

Mateo's face fell and his voice quieted. "Izzy, you must have dreamed it."

"No! He was here with me. He told me what was written on the baseball." I set Frida on the ground and reached into my pocket. "It's gone!"

"What? What's gone?"

"My baseball. I had it." I patted my pocket as if I could have missed it the first time. Frantically, I scanned the ground.

Mateo hung his head. "It probably fell in the river, Izzy." He tugged at my arm. "We can find it in the morning."

"No! It's special. You don't understand."

I ran up and down the river's edge searching. "Please help me, Dad." I murmured. The water tumbled along as if nothing had ever happened.

Mateo followed behind me, searching under bushes and rocks and the last bit of moonlight hid behind a long cloud. It seemed impossible now to find it in the muddy dark.

But before I could take my next breath, Frida bounded toward me wagging her tail and carrying my ball in her mouth as if we'd been playing a game of fetch. How she ever got her small jaws around it is a mystery.

I dropped to my knees and eased the ball from her mouth, whispering, "Good dog." She stood on her hind legs and licked my cheek. I lifted her into my arms.

"She found it," I called to Mateo a few feet away. "Frida found it."

Within seconds Mateo stood in front of me, scratching Frida's back. Her mouth parted in a dog grinning way. "Good job, girl."

Mateo's eyes met mine. "What now?"

"I have to see Socorro. I have to tell her what happened."
I turned and hiked up the riverbank carrying Frida, my baseball, and an armful of dread.

24

MAGGIE'S STORY

A glow shone though Socorro's front gate like a distant lighthouse guiding me home. Somehow I knew she was expecting me.

As we approached her front door, I turned to Mateo. "Could you wait outside?"

He took Frida from my arms. "Sure."

Before I could knock, the front door opened and Socorro reached out her arms to hug me. "You have been through quite an ordeal haven't you?"

"Maggie is hurt and—"

"I know, Izzy."

"She's going to come home soon, right?"

"I don't know."

My heart caught in my throat. "But why? I thought you were a seer."

"I may see things that are to happen, but I can't always control what I see."

Socorro led me to a small sofa in the living room. "Please, sit and I will make you some tea."

I cupped my head in my hands and dragged my hands down my face. I wanted Socorro to fix it. She returned with a tray of tea and set it before me on the pine table. She poured me a cup and I watched the steam rise in swirls.

"Why did I have to be so stupid? Please tell me she'll be fine."

She stood and walked across the room to the window. "Remember the story I told you? Do you want to hear the ending now?"

I nodded.

"Once the girl showed her family the silver, the whole town soon knew about the treasure. Then one night, a thief stole it while the family slept. Everyone was saddened by their loss. They believed they had nothing left and would never be able to rebuild their home."

She took a sip of tea.

"But what does it mean?" I asked.

Socorro's eyes softened and she set her tea on the table. "You must find the answer for yourself."

"So did they rebuild their home?"

"Of course with the silver it would have been easier, but after many, many years of hard work they did rebuild it."

Tía and Mr. Castillo were pacing under the back portal when Mateo and I arrived back at Nana's house.

"*Gracias a Dios!*" Tía dashed toward me and Mateo in a long pink robe and hair curlers. "When Nana left here, she was frantic." Tía made a sign of the cross, her face streaked with black mascara.

I nuzzled my face into her neck. She smelled of freshly washed towels.

"They took Maggie to the hospital," Mateo said.

Mr. Castillo's eyes drooped more than usual. He gazed at both of us. "Are you two okay?"

Mateo nodded and I wiped my face with both hands.

Tía squeezed my shoulder lightly. "Nana told us to wait here in case your mama called back."

"Has she?" I said.

Tía glanced at Mr. Castillo and back at me. "Not yet, *mija*. But your nana said she sounded very worried."

Mr. Castillo patted Mateo's back. "You two should get some rest. In the morning everything will be better."

That night, everyone slept on Nana's side of the house—Tía and Mr. Castillo in one of the guest rooms and Mateo on the couch.

As I walked toward Estrella, I ran my fingers along the *santos* on the walls and whispered prayers: a prayer for forgiveness, a prayer for Maggie. A painting of *la familia sagrada* hung right outside my bedroom door. I stopped in front of the framed picture and stared at the faces of Mary, Joseph, and Jesus.

"Please bless Maggie. Give me a sign she'll be home soon," I whispered and made the sign of the cross.

The three faces just stared back, as solemn as before. I pressed open the heavy wooden door to my room. I blinked and stepped inside to get a closer look. My story cards were tied together with Maggie's yarn and hung delicately from the light fixture in the center of the room. They looked like creamy clouds inching across the sky. Had Maggie done all this?

"I helped her with it." Tía stood in the doorway.

"She used all her yarn for me? What about her ladder to heaven?"

"She was so upset about breaking your truth catcher. We spent hours threading and hanging the cards. She said they had to be connected so you could write a story."

Tía smiled softly. "She loves you like a sister, Izzy."

I nodded and whispered, "I love her too."

As Tía closed the door I climbed up on my bed and ran my hand through the floating story cards. Each one held strings of words that needed a place to belong. But one stood out among them all: Maggie's card. The one where she wrote *Flyeng Princis*.

I took a stack of blank story cards and wrote across the top one: *Maggie's Story, by Izzy* and as I began to write Roybal, my hand swept across the card and looped into a *B* and I wrote *Bella*.

I liked the way *Bella* looked on paper and I finished it off by writing *Reed Roybal*. Staring at the card I realized Mom had given me two pieces of my name and so had Dad.

With the pen in hand, I set my baseball on the desk and ever so carefully wrote in the missing words, beginning with the loop of the *L* for love.

Because love is magic.

Now the baseball was complete. Suddenly, I felt a warm tingle up my spine and down my right arm and the pen in my hand began to move as Maggie's princess story unfolded. I wrote every detail as it came to me and before I knew it I had a stack of cards filled with words.

The one-winged angel on the wall seemed to wink down at me.

"I wrote my first story," I whispered. "For Maggie."

A breeze drifted through the window and brushed my face. I grabbed a sapphire blue pencil from the desk drawer and jumped onto the bed. "If you really are a guardian angel, could you watch over Maggie now?"

Slowly, I traced the pencil across the plaster wall and drew a wide open wing on the right side of the angel reaching toward heaven. "There. That should help you fly a little faster."

25

A Sign from Heaven

A few hours later, the sun rose over the majestic Sandias, washing Nana's house in pink light. When Nana arrived home at lunch time, sadness draped across her shoulders, and she looked even smaller than usual.

"How's Maggie?" I asked, my voice barely a whisper.

Nana sat by the Santa Maria altar and lit two small candles. The pink morning light crossed her face as she turned to me, and for a moment it looked like she was happy. But just as quickly, the candle light flickered, casting shadows across her stony face, and I saw the truth.

"The doctors say there is nothing wrong with her, but she won't wake up. So all we can do is wait." She rubbed her hand across her brow.

I kneeled in front of her. "Nana, I am so sorry. I didn't mean for any of this to happen. I was just so tired of waiting and—"

Nana held up her hand signaling for me to stop talking. "Gip entrusted Maggie to me, and now I have let her down."

"No. This is my fault. I thought if I could just talk to my dad that everything would be clear. Please forgive me."

"I have already forgiven you. I see your intentions were good. But sometimes we must stop thinking of ourselves and think of others."

"I know. That's why I need to see Maggie."

Nothing could have prepared me for the ashen whisper of a girl Maggie had become. The pale edges of her face sank low, leaving her cheeks hollow and frail. The small white room smelled like my last school after the janitors had pushed their blackened mops around the hallways.

"Hi, Maggie," I whispered. "I brought you a gift."

I longed to hear her small voice. To watch her braids bounce across her back sack. To feel her soft hands around my waist.

I hung her back sack on a shelf near the bed so she could see it when she woke up. Burying my face in the side of the bed, I set my hand on her arm. "I'm sorry, Maggie. I should never have been so selfish. I was only thinking about myself. But I wrote a story for you, the one where you're the princess."

Holding a stack of cards in one hand I read my words.

"Once there was an invisible girl from nowhere, who became friends with a princess from an enchanted forest. The princess was magic because she was one of the few people who could see the invisible girl. They listened to ghost stories and searched for treasure and soon they became sisters. But one day the little princess left the enchanted forest. Her sister searched for her night and day but couldn't find her.

"She asked the stars, 'Have you seen my sister?'

"They told her they hadn't. Then she asked the moon, 'Have you seen my sister?'

"The moon had no reply. She sat under a tree and wept. Then the wind came by and she asked the wind, 'Have you seen my sister?'

"The wind replied, 'She has taken a special ladder to heaven.'

"'But how did she get there?' the girl asked.

"'She flew.'

"The next day, the invisible girl waited for the princess to fly down from the heavens. But each day the sun set and the moon appeared and the princess did not come home. The invisible girl decided she needed magic to bring her sister home, but she didn't have any. All she had was love. That night she climbed the highest tree and sent her love on the tail of the strongest wind.

"The next sunrise, the princess flew down from the sky. The invisible girl threw her arms around her welcoming her home."

I stroked Maggie's small fingers and smiled. "And the invisible girl wasn't invisible ever again."

When Nana and I got home that day, someone stood in the backyard herb garden. Walking toward the window for a closer look my heart skipped a beat. Was it really her?

"Mom!" I threw open the backdoor and ran toward her.

Mom ran to me with her arms open wide. "Izzy. I was so scared." She held me at arm's length and eyed me up and down, worry in her eyes. She pulled me to her tightly, like she hadn't seen me in a century. "Thank God."

Fresh tears sprung from my eyes. I nestled into her arms and we stood together for a long time. Finally, Mom stepped back and looked over my shoulder. "Hi, Mama."

"It is good to see you, *mija*," Nana said.

They embraced and cried.

Mom tucked her hair behind her ear and turned back to me. "I am just so grateful you weren't hurt. I don't think I could bear . . ."

Mom folded her arms across her chest as we eased into the chairs under the portal. "Izzy, so much has changed. I was wrong. I didn't see it . . ." She took a deep breath. "Somehow, Costa Rica brought me closer to my roots."

I examined her face, her eyes, her mouth. Dad had loved her. And she had lost something too.

She continued. "The way the moon hung low across the jungle. It felt magical. Like the village."

Nana leaned across the table and patted Mom's hand.

"A flood of memories washed over me there, memories I couldn't run from anymore." She paused, turning her face to the sun. "I remembered those nights when we hiked the valley together. Remember, Mama?"

Nana laughed through her tears. "I remember."

Mom leaned back and took a long deep breath, like breathing in fresh-baked *empanadas*. "I have missed this place." She reached for my hand. "Come on. Let's take a walk."

Before we left, I grabbed my canvas bag from the house and tossed the ball inside.

We strolled down the trails of the village toward the edge of the river. I listened to the sound of the rushing waters. The sun floated across the middle of the sky making its descent into the west. Mom led me to a patch of soft earth near the river's edge where we nestled under a small tree.

"He loved you so much, Izzy. He would be proud of you." Tears rolled gently down her face.

I plucked a dandelion from the ground and twisted it between my fingers, letting her words settle inside me.

"That's what he said." I avoided Mom's eyes, afraid she might not believe me.

"What who said?"

"The night at the river. I woke up on the riverbank, but . . . first I went . . ." I glanced at Mom's face. She was still listening. "I saw Dad."

Mom placed her head on my shoulder and sighed. "I visit him in my dreams too."

I drew back and searched her eyes. "No, it wasn't a dream. He was there."

"Where?"

Pulling my knees into my chest, I said, "A visiting place."

She stroked my hair and pressed her lips together as though she was deciding whether it was true. Whether she should believe me. Mom's voice quivered. "There is a village myth of such a place."

"He told me about the words on the baseball," I said.

Recognition flashed across her face.

Words spilled from my mouth as I reached into the bag and pulled the ball out. "I took it from the box. I'm sorry."

Mom scanned the words written across the ball. She choked back a sob. "'Because Love is Magic.' How could you know?"

Blinking back tears I whispered, "He told me to ask you. That you'd tell me."

Mom's bewildered eyes darted back and forth across my face. She took a deep breath and searched the distance like she would find the right words somewhere on the horizon. "He asked me to marry him right before a championship game. I only laughed and told him we were too young. But in my deepest heart I wanted to say yes."

"Then what happened?"

"He asked again and still I said no. I told him I needed a sign. A sign from heaven." Mom rolled her eyes. "I don't know why. I knew I would say yes. But it was too much fun teasing him."

I leaned forward, not wanting to miss one word.

"He said that if he could hit a home run on his first time up to bat that night, it would be a sign."

Mom stroked her fingers through my hair. "I told him he was crazy. How could he control that? Actually I kind of worried he wouldn't be able to and then I'd have to say no for sure. 'How do you know you can?' I asked him. He smiled that perfect smile and said, 'Because love is magic.'" She took a deep breath and smiled. "And he did it."

"You must've been so sad when he died. I'm sorry, Mom."

In the distance, hues of gold and pink melted into the mountain range, casting a watermelon glow.

"How did the words get erased?"

Mom shrugged. "I have no idea. He didn't play with it again after the home run. Maybe they wore off over time? All that matters is you know the truth and the words are back where they belong."

We sat in silence listening to the gurgling river and the soft wind stirring the trees.

She patted my hand and said, "Do you have any other questions?"

"He named me Bella?" I whispered.

She brushed her hair from her face and wiped her tears. "Your father loved the name Bella. We'd called you that from the time I became pregnant." She shook her head and choked back the tears. "But once he was gone, I just couldn't call you by that name every day. I needed to forget. But it's still your name if you want to keep it."

"I do." I laughed and rolled my eyes. "Sorry, Mom, but Isadora? It's so old-fashioned."

She laughed too.

"You can still call me Izzy for short, but Isabella is a good writer's name. Don't you think?"

"Yes. Very writerly," Mom nodded.

I picked at the wild grass. "My name is the only thing Dad ever gave me."

"No." Mom hugged me. "He gave you his heart. His way of seeing the world and all its magic."

I leaned toward the melting sun.

"And now I see that it wasn't an accident I got that funding to go away. You were meant to come here this summer. I guess in my heart I knew you'd find the truth. I just didn't think I could be the one to tell you, and I'm so sorry."

"I understand, Mom."

We sat in silence for another moment before she said, "It's not your fault, Izzy. What happened to Maggie had nothing to do with you. Just like your father's death wasn't my fault. For a long time I blamed myself." She rested her hand on mine. "But you know what I've learned? That sometimes we can't explain how life happens. Life unfolds exactly as it is meant to, in just the right time and place."

I brushed the grass with my fingertips.

She squeezed my hand. "Are you glad you came after all?"

I nodded. "You were right when you said I'd be surprised. And that it's strange and beautiful here." A light wind swirled all around us and I smiled.

"I have missed that sight." Mom sighed as she stared across the valley. "It's good to finally be home. For good."

The distant sun spread a brilliant rosy hue across the sky, like a warm blanket before the night pushes out the light. I felt small under the sky, but in my mother's arms I felt safe.

Mom stood and stretched. "You ready?"

"Not yet. I want to be alone for a minute."

Mom headed back to the village, leaving me alone. Only a sliver of blushing sky lingered.

I was lost in my own thoughts as I strolled down the path home, thinking about how much my life had changed over summer.

"Hi, Izzy." Mateo stepped from the shadows and leaned against the tree. A wave of dark hair hung over his eye. "I brought you some *empanadas*." He handed me a brown paper sack tied at the top with blue ribbon. "I'm sorry I didn't believe you about your dad."

I squished the paper sack in the palm of my hand. "It probably sounded pretty crazy. Want one?" I held out the sack.

He laughed nervously. "I already ate a few. So, have you heard any more about Maggie?"

"Not yet. But I really want to do something special for her . . . when she comes home."

"Like what?"

"I have an idea, but I'm not sure if it will work."

"What? Tell me."

"I think I have a way for her to take her ladder to heaven. To give the yarn back to her mom."

"Let me guess, you want me to grow wings, right?" he teased.

"Actually, that's not too far off."

Mateo looked confused. "I was just kidding."

I stepped closer and told him my plan for Maggie. "So you think it'll work?"

Mateo's dark shiny eyes searched my face. "It's perfect," he murmured, but why was he looking at me that way? My stomach did a little flip.

Inching backward, I stumbled over a branch and Mateo grabbed hold of my arm.

And that's when it happened.

He leaned in and kissed me. And as he did, I closed my eyes and felt the world tilting beneath me.

26

TORTILLA SUN

The next morning, Nana's voice jolted me from my sleep. "*Qué milagro!*"

I jumped out of bed and ran to the living room with Frida prancing a step ahead of me.

"Nana, what are you doing here? I thought you spent the night at the hospital."

She wrapped her arms around my waist and danced me around the room, laughing and crying at the same time. "Our prayers have been answered. She is coming home!"

Mom ran into the room tugging at the belt on her robe. "What's all this about, Mama?"

My heart soared. "Maggie is coming home, Mom!"

Nana gripped our hands creating a circle. "Early this morning, I was just getting ready to come home for a rest when she opened her eyes and spoke to me." She clapped her hands together and laughed. "She said she was hungry!"

"When can I see her?" I asked now wide awake.

"The doctors want to run a few more tests today—so no visitors—but if all goes well, tomorrow."

Frida bounced toward the door as if she understood that Maggie was coming home. "You're not going anywhere." I chuckled. "She'll be home soon." It was when I bent down and hoisted her over my shoulder that I noticed it was gone.

The last scrap of black crepe had disappeared.

Twenty-four hours can seem like a lifetime when you're waiting for something important. But that's how long I had to wait to see Maggie. I chiseled those hours away in the kitchen cooking with Mom. We kept busy preparing all of Maggie's favorite foods—strawberries dipped in sugar, bean burritos, red chile *enchiladas* and *sopaipillas* filled with tomatoes and cheese.

Mom told me all about Dad. "Your dad had a great sense of humor, always had to put his left shoe on first, loved animals, had a crooked smile, lived for strawberry ice cream rolled in *tortillas,* and believed he could save the world one person at a time." I ate up the details of my father's life like bits of warm *tortilla* soaked in honey.

When I heard the car roll across the crushed gravel in the driveway, I bolted from the kitchen into the living room. "She's here!"

I stood at the screen door and watched Maggie walk slowly across the courtyard. Frida was right behind, wagging her tail with all her might.

"Maggie!" I opened the door and nearly tumbled on top of her. She backed up laughing.

"*¿Tienes hambre?*" Nana asked Maggie as she inched her way past us.

"Starved," Maggie said.

"What do you want—ice cream, cookies, *pan dulce?* Anything you want." Nana smiled.

Maggie narrowed her eyes at me. "I want one of Izzy's *tortillas* and I want it round like the sun."

"You know you're asking for the impossible, right?" I said smiling.

Maggie kissed the top of Frida's head. "Frida wants one too, right Frida?" She moved Frida's head up and down.

Nana followed me into the kitchen while Maggie and Mom waited in the living room.

I measured the ingredients with Nana watching carefully. She took my hands and helped me press the dough.

"*Sí, sí* that's it, *mija*, it has only been practice up until now and you had to practice to learn the basics. But now you are ready." She handed me the amber bottle.

"How does the secret ingredient work?"

"That," she said pointing her finger to the ceiling, "is the secret."

I squeezed her small frame and smiled. I guess some secrets are meant to be kept. "I love you, Nana."

I sprinkled out some of the contents of the amber bottle just like she had shown me, and began to round out the edges. Slowly, the *tortilla* began to take shape. Rounder and rounder it grew until I was done. I stood back and stared in disbelief. I had done it: a perfect circle. "I can't pick it up."

"You must pick it up."

"But what if it falls apart?"

"Then you will start again."

I peeled the edges carefully, hoping they wouldn't stick to the board. Each section of the dough lifted up without resistance. I placed it on the *comal* as if it were a fine piece of china. The dough bubbled and browned.

I counted, *1, 2, 3, 4—turn, 1, 2, 3, 4—turn*. And held up the hot *tortilla* for Nana to see. "I did it! I did it!"

There in her magical kitchen we laughed like we hadn't in weeks.

"Look." She beamed. "A perfect *tortilla* sun."

I carried the batch in a *tortilla* basket and stood tall in front of Maggie. "First one on top goes to you. A *tortilla* sun, *princesa*." I knelt like a knight in a fairytale.

Maggie tore off a piece of the *tortilla* and handed it to Frida, who gobbled it up.

That night, Maggie crawled under the bed and came back out with something tucked under her shirt.

"What is it?" I asked.

She lifted her T-shirt and pulled out a round piece of yellow colored glass, covered in cracks, but intact.

"My truth catcher! How did you put it back together?"

"When you left that day, me and your nana got all the pieces in a pile. Then we just glued 'em together with super glue. It was like doing a puzzle. You wanna hang it back up?"

I studied the remade truth catcher. None of the pieces were an exact fit with the next and yet it was perfect.

Kneeling down, I hugged Maggie tight. I held the truth catcher by its long yellow ribbon and hung it in front of the window. The morning sunlight cast a hundred tiny rainbows through the prisms of glass.

A constellation of dancing lights spread across the floor. I gasped, and pointed to the *Saltillo* floor. "Maggie do you see that?"

"The rainbow?"

I bounced across the room toward the colorful rays of light. "It looks like the village."

Maggie knelt down for a closer look.

I pointed toward the image. "See the pink lines? That's the church, see the cross? And look at the blue. It's the river. And the center of the village, with the *adobes* all around is a perfect square."

Maggie waved her hand in front of my face. "Are you crazy, Izzy? 'Cause I can't see anything but a bunch of little rainbows."

I grabbed a pencil and traced the lines across the tile. I stepped back and removed the truth catcher from the window. There on the floor was a rough sketch of the village.

Maggie pressed her small hand to her mouth and giggled. "That's cheating. You drew that."

"Now do you see it?" I smiled to myself and whispered, "It's home."

27

RIDING THE SKIES

Nana's backyard soon swarmed with visitors and well-wishers. Mom talked and laughed with old friends, catching up on all that she'd missed. Every once in a while her eyes would grow wide with surprise and she'd say, "You're kidding!" Like it was the most amazing thing she'd ever heard.

I stood alone beneath the cottonwood in the middle of the yard, watching the party from a distance. Someone tapped my shoulder and I turned to find Socorro standing in front of me in a soft yellow sundress. Long turquoise earrings dangled from her ears.

"Hi, Socorro."

"Are you enjoying the *fiesta*?"

I nodded. We stood together in silence watching the villagers.

"I know what the story means now."

She smoothed her dress. Her sage eyes glistened in the afternoon sun.

"The family from the story only cared about what they didn't have instead of focusing on what they did have. Everything wasn't completely gone. They still had part of their home, the floor. And they didn't realize that maybe they could rebuild their home without the silver even though it would be harder," I said.

Socorro studied my face. "Sometimes we long for what the world tells us is missing, and miss what is right in front of us."

I watched Maggie blow bubbles across the lawn for Frida. "I want to thank you."

"For what?"

"I let my story simmer, like you said, and I wrote one. From beginning to end." Two bubbles floated toward me, suspended on the breeze.

Socorro side-hugged me and said, "You're welcome. Now go finish your surprise for Maggie. And maybe you'll find your own surprise."

⌒

After we finished eating, Mateo and I led Maggie to the mesa above the village.

"Where are we going?" she asked every two minutes as we wound through the trees.

"It's a surprise. Now close your eyes. We're almost there," I said.

When we arrived on the flat desert above the river, I said, "Now you can open 'em."

Maggie opened her blue eyes and squealed. "Are we gonna ride it?" she asked, her eyes wide with surprise.

"It's our chariot for the day," Mateo said smiling.

Red flames shot like a hundred dragons' tongues into a blue hot air balloon. Pictures of big, billowy clouds stretched all around it, blending into the perfect summer sky. Maggie hopped up and down from one foot to the other while the flames filled the balloon with windy gusts of hot air.

"Look, Izzy. We get to float near heaven!"

I squeezed her small hand and smiled. We settled into the basket with Mr. Castillo, and within a moment, the balloon lurched forward; a blast of fire and wind and we lifted off the ground, rising into the July sky.

Maggie laughed. "That tickled my tummy."

The ground fell away as the balloon rose higher and higher. We soared high above the earth, like a puffy cloud inching across the sky.

"Hey Maggie, we brought you a present. Actually it's the reason for the balloon." I pulled her yarn from the canvas bag.

Maggie pulled the ladder from my hands. She looked up toward Mateo. "It's a ladder! You made this for me?"

"It was Izzy's idea."

Maggie reached up toward my ear with her hand cupped on the left side of her mouth. I bent down toward her as she whispered, "Do you think she'll catch it?"

I nodded and smiled.

She smiled a gap-toothed grin and leaned over the edge of the basket. Closing her eyes she tossed the ladder into the wind. "Now Mommy can have her yarn back."

The yarn drifted across the breeze, staying aloft as long as we could see it.

Faint, slow whispers clung to the breeze and as we rose higher the wind spoke clearer. *Tesoro.* Treasure. I turned my face to the wind and imagined Dad riding the skies in this balloon, loving the wind in his face, and the whispers on the breeze. We were the same that way. Just as I'd always imagined.

We climbed higher and higher into the heavens, and the clouds seemed close enough to touch. Maggie reached her hands out toward the sky.

"What are you doing?" I asked.

"I want a piece of a cloud."

Mateo laughed. "You can't catch clouds, Maggie."

Maggie's face fell.

"Sure you can," I said. "Give me your hand."

Maggie placed her hand in mine and I stretched it out toward the softest one in the sky. For just a moment the clouds seemed to stand still.

"Now close your eyes and picture that cloud right in the center of your palm." I waited a moment. "Is it there yet?"

She nodded.

"Good." I held open her back sack and said, "Now put it in here so you can take it home, and remember, you might not be able to see it but you can feel it. Like magic."

Gazing at the village below, I blinked twice before I was sure. And then, I was so sure I shouted, "Mateo, do you see that?" I pointed toward the northern part of the village. "It's the B from the map. See? Those bushes form a perfect B." I laughed. "And remember the map said something about soaring with fire?"

Mateo's eyes darted across the earth below. He reached into his pocket and pulled out the map. He read the directions, "'There you must soar with fire, to see the treasure you desire.' Izzy, you're right! I can't believe it. We only needed a new view to see it. Do you really think there's a treasure down there?"

I gazed toward the village, my home, and smiled. "I'm sure of it."

ACKNOWLEDGMENTS

With loving gratitude to my mom, Anna, for giving me my first words, roots to keep me grounded, and wings to help me fly—you saw the light before I did; to my entire family for their love and encouragement; to my husband, Joseph, for giving me the freedom to explore the Land of Enchantment; to Alex for being the head plotmeister even during football season; to Bella for keeping Maggie alive and giving me cooler words than I could have thought up alone; and to my Julie Bear for asking me to write her a story and for reading it through in one sitting.

Special thanks to Laurie McLean, agent extraordinaire, who believed in a first-time author and who, thank goodness, was hungry the day she read the manuscript; to my tireless editor, Julie Romeis, for saying yes, and taking the time to unfold the story and excavate the magic from the pages; to everyone at Chronicle for being committed to creating a special book.

Many thanks to my generous critique partners, David (for re-reading chapters on short notice and helping me make them shine), Louise, Loretta, and Andi, for their generosity; to Char/Lena for keeping me sane during the revision process with good humor and great writing.

And in remembrance of my grandmothers, Gertrude and Priscilla: Thank you for giving me Nana.

Author's Note

When I was a young girl, I spent time in the natural beauty of the New Mexican desert. My grandmother's house was nestled among cottonwood trees where the rhythm of the cicada bugs hummed me to sleep on dreamy summer nights. Her tiny kitchen was filled with the sweet aromas of Mexican spices and homemade *tortillas*. There was something timeless about her kitchen. Perhaps it represented a moment long drawn out by the hustle and bustle of our modern hurried life or a place where magic still existed for those who believed. Today, I challenge you to slow time to a stroll and make a batch of homemade *tortillas*. I have included the recipe my grandmother used, although there may be a secret ingredient left out, but maybe you can create your own as you make your very own *tortilla* sun!

NANA'S FLOUR TORTILLAS

YIELDS 12 TORTILLAS

4   cups (510 grams) all-purpose flour

1½ teaspoons salt

2   teaspoons baking powder

4   tablespoons (55 grams) lard or shortening (sometimes
    my grandmother used bacon grease for this)

1½ cups (360 millilitres) warm water

Combine dry ingredients in a mixing bowl. Use a fork to cut the shortening into the dry ingredients, or do it like Nana and just use your hands. Make a well in the center and slowly add the water to form the dough. Knead as you add water to incorporate and make the dough. Knead the dough in the bowl until it is smooth. Remember, no stickies. Cover the bowl with wax paper and set aside for ten minutes.

Form the dough into small balls and flatten between your palms. Sprinkle a little bit of flour onto a smooth surface. With a rolling pin, roll each ball into a 6-inch (15-centimetre) circle, or whatever shape yours turn into at first (this part takes lots of practice and they'll taste just as good if they turn out looking like Texas). Remember to roll from the center out. Lift the dough and turn with each roll.

Heat a *comal* or cast-iron skillet on the stove for two to three minutes on medium to high heat. Cook *tortillas* on the *comal*, usually one to two minutes on each side. They should have brown speckles all over.

Drizzle with butter, tuck in the bottom end, roll and enjoy! Place the remainder of the cooked *tortillas* in between wax paper and place in a large resealable plastic bag for another day. If well-sealed, they should keep for two weeks.

Glossary

Adiós	Good-bye
Amiga	Female friend
Apúrate	Hurry up
Bonita	Pretty
Buenos días	Good Morning
Burrito	A flour tortilla wrapped around a filling, usually beans, rice, and meat
Caballeros	Slang term for a cowboy
Chile Relleno	A stuffed chile that is fried in egg batter
Cielo	Heaven/sky
Ciudad	City
Comida	Food
Cuento	Story
De nada	You're welcome
Descanso	Memorial that honors the place of a loved one's death
El café	Coffee
Empanada	A stuffed bread or pastry
Enchilada	Tortilla filled with meat or cheese and baked in chili sauce
Exactamente	Exactly
Fiesta	Party
Gracias	Thank you
Gracias a Dios	Thank God
¿Hablas Español?	Do you speak Spanish?
Hola	Hi

La Familia Sagrada	The Sacred Family
Loca	Crazy
Mañana	Tomorrow
Mariachi	A certain type of musical group popular in Mexico.
Mi casa es su casa	My house is your house
Mija/Mijita	Affectionate term for daughter or little girl
Mira	Look
Música	Music
Muy bien	Very good
Panadería	Bakery
Pan dulce	Sweet bread
Piñata	Decorated papier mâché container filled with candy
Sagrada	Sacred
Saltillo	Mexican floor tile
Santa Ana	Mother of Mary, grandmother of Jesus
Santo	Saint
Señorita	Young lady
Sí	Yes
Sígame	Follow me
Sopaipilla	Puffy, deep-fried pastry often served with honey or syrup
Taco	A corn or flour tortilla wrapped around a filling, often beef or chicken
Tamale	Traditional Latin American dish consisting of steam-cooked corn dough (masa) filled with various foods (pork, beef, chicken)
¿Tienes hambre?	Are you hungry?
Un momento	One moment
Ven	Come